Queen of
Hearts

Also by Vera and Bill Cleaver

Queen of Hearts

VERA AND BILL CLEAVER

HarperTrophy

A Division of HarperCollins*Publishers*

Library of Congress Cataloging in Publication Data

Cleaver, Vera.
   Queen of hearts.

   SUMMARY: Although there is no love lost between
them, twelve-year-old Wilma is her wilful and peppery
grandmother's choice for a companion.
   [1. Grandmothers—Fiction.   2. Old age—Fiction.   3. Family
life—Fiction]   I. Cleaver, Bill, joint author.   II. Title.
PZ7.C57926Que   [Fic]   77-18252
ISBN 0-397-31771-9

   "A Harper Trophy book"
ISBN 0-06-440196-0 (pbk.)

First Harper Trophy edition, 1987

To Mama

———————————————

Queen of
Hearts

One

At twelve years of age Wilma Omalie Lincoln was not a great thinker or a great anything, a condition that was satisfactory to herself as well as her parents. A large, sloppy child whose blood ran to a pastel kind of indifference, she had straight brown hair and perpetual question marks for eyebrows, though whether the world had meaning or was meaningless had never stirred a great to-do in her mind. Her emotions had never been called upon to make any big responses, and thus her private self had a government of its own, calm and detached. She owned a black felt hat decorated with a long pheasant's tail that had once been the property of her grandmother Lincoln and two plastic six-shooters painted gunmetal gray to make them look real, and she spent a good deal of her free time in the hardwood hammocks and piny flatwoods surrounding Timberlake, her north Florida town.

Wilma's make-believe companions were two soldiers of fortune (neither of them had any personal interest in her); an escaped convict on his way to the bedside of his dying mother (his crime was only petty larceny); an international spy (female); a Greek sponge diver who had once been a shotgun lookout for a stagecoach line out of Abilene, Kansas; a couple of trappers; and one bird fancier. Her real companion was Claybrook, her six-year-old brother. He was one of those jumpy little kids who always had to be busy at something.

Claybrook's powers of imagination were passionless. They weren't worth a cuss. He understood not a one of her harmless ghost-friends. He could not comprehend the word picture she painted for him of the bitter and treacherous wilderness, never saw the swaying, creaking stagecoach moving through the dark line of the distant trees, the wounded driver still clinging desperately to her box of gold and the horses' reins and yelling to her passengers to, "Keep your heads in, fools! There's more trouble ahead!"

Claybrook didn't care much for the international spy or the soldiers or the trappers either. The Greek sponge diver and the bird fancier he ignored. He always wanted to be somewhere he wasn't. He was never comfortable. "Let's go back home, Wilma. I'm cold."

Said Wilma, "If you'd eat something once in a while you wouldn't be cold all the time, you skinny little wart. It's June. How can you be cold?"

"You didn't give me time to eat my breakfast."

"I gave you as much time as I gave myself."

"I'm cold."

"You want my hat?"

"No. It smells bad."

"It'd keep your head warm."

"I don't want it."

"You want to play some cards?"

"No. You always cheat."

"I won't this time. Look, here's a new deck. It hasn't even been opened. Let's play some cards. I'll let you win this time."

"I don't want to. I want to go back home."

"What for? There's no more to do there than there is here."

"Let's go see Granny."

"Granny doesn't want to see us. We give her nervous snits. She's busy with her own stuff. We're not supposed to go to her house unless she invites us."

"Maybe today she forgot to invite us."

"She didn't. Granny never forgets anything."

"I'm going to see her," said Claybrook, springing one of his clever, two-edged decisions. "If she tells me to go home I'll do it."

By this time the bitter and treacherous wilderness was sunlit. Immediately about, all was quietude and peace and emptiness. The early morning ground fog had disappeared, as had the phantom stagecoach and all the spectral participants in this favored creation.

Wilma was not without a sense of stoic responsibility, so presently she and Claybrook left the woods and went to see Granny Lincoln, who lived in a house four streets over from theirs. Granny was seventy-nine, equipped with an active brain, a hardy little body, and a free will. She viewed her ability to live her widow's life by herself in her paid-for home as an advantage over others her age, all those good-old-days whiners who sat and rocked, who waited for their daughters and sons and grandchildren to come. And when they didn't, wept.

Granny never talked about the good old days except to say, "They were a lot of hee-haw, same as they are now." To cross her in any of her opinions or to suggest changes in any of her habits was more dangerous than gargling with household bleach. Her street, which was a short cul-de-sac, contained only four houses, two of them vacant. Her neighbor was Mr. Ben Frost. Not Benjamin, but just plain Ben.

"Because," explained Ben, droll and old and prankish, "I was born on a washday. Back in the time when I came along people didn't have time to look through classy books for fancy names for their kids. They just grabbed one, and the shorter the better."

Ben's wife was dead and he waited for no one to come visit him because there was no one. He washed his own clothes, cleaned his own house, and cooked his own meals. On Sundays he rigged himself out in whatever garb best suited his mood, phoned for a taxi to come, and sallied off to the church of his faith. He owned a car but in the eyes of Florida law wasn't healthy enough to drive it, so the vehicle, relic of a world that had changed too fast for Ben Frost, sat in his closed garage. The only reason Ben went to church for Sunday meetings was to argue with the preacher. For that same purpose he never missed prayer meetings on Wednesday evenings either.

This was a Tuesday, and as Wilma and Claybrook passed Ben's house his front door opened and he stepped out onto his porch. He called out to them. "Hey, Wilma. . . . Hey, Claybrook. Where's the fire?"

"We're going to see Granny," said Claybrook.

Said Ben, "I don't think she's up yet. I haven't seen her this morning. Her paper's still in her yard. Wilma, did the chief of police ever make you a special deputy so you could wear them guns legally?" He hid his mirthless laughter with his sleeve. "Woop. Woop."

Old cockroach, thought Wilma. I was eight when I told him about wanting to be a special deputy. He's just like all the rest. You slip up and tell them one little bitty fraud about yourself and forever after they neigh and bray like some silly hinny with his brains knocked out every time they see you. She said, "Hey, Ben. How you feeling?"

Answered Ben, "Pretty good, if you don't ask for details."

"What details?" asked Claybrook, exhibiting a blank curiosity.

"Claybrook," said Wilma, "you go ahead on. Tell Granny I'll be there in a minute. Take her her paper. Tell her we were just passing by and thought we'd stop in for a second." She could tell by the look on Ben's face that he had a mind full of details and wasn't going to let her get away before he had dumped at least half of them on her. Ben always had details. She watched Claybrook cut through Ben's yard and enter Granny's.

Ben was descending his steps. When he reached the bottom one he sat down. Self-educated, a retired rancher originally from the central part of the state, he was eighty-three and believed that snakes had pouches on the sides of their heads for their babies to jump into when scared. He said, "We had some excitement here last evenin'. A kid on a motorcycle ran into one of those little cars. Your granny and I were standing out there by the curb talking and we witnessed the whole thing."

Wilma said, "Granny will tell me all about it, Ben."

"It was the kid's fault," continued Ben. "When the police got here we told them what happened, and guess what they said?"

"What?" asked Wilma.

"They wanted to know how old we were," replied Ben, and laughed his rickety laugh. "And then your granny got mad and asked them how old they were."

"Did anybody get hurt?" inquired Wilma.

"No," said Ben. "It wasn't that kind of accident. The police gave the man driving the car a ticket and the kid climbed back on his motor thing and rode off and then your granny and me each got a broom and went out and cleaned up the glass."

"Is that all?" asked Wilma.

"You don't get it, do you?" said Ben.

"It was an accident," said Wilma.

"Yes," agreed Ben. "An accident." He had run out of details, seemed to have forgotten her. He had dropped his head forward and was studying his slippered feet as if they were some new addition to himself.

I bet it didn't even happen, thought Wilma, annoyed with Ben but more so with herself, because hidden somewhere in the story just recited to her there was meaning beyond her fathoming. She hitched the belt containing the two holstered six-shooters so that it settled to a more comfortable position around her waist. How was it that all of her encounters with Ben left her with a feeling of being dwarfed and guilty? As if, within her person, she carried something that did not quite wholly belong to her. Why could she never take leave of him easily? She owed him nothing. It wasn't as if he was so poor he couldn't hire somebody to come listen to all his silly scarecrow details. According to Granny he had thousands of dollars stashed away in the First National Bank of Timberlake. Old cockroach. Wilma said, "Ben, I've got to go now."

Ben raised his head and looked at her. His eyes went past her to the waste field on the opposite side of the street where creeper vines of rattan and wild grape grew in the hammock jungle. Dismissing her, he said, "I got to go too. Got a date with a hardware store. Need me some new light bulbs."

A minute later Wilma stood beside Claybrook on Granny Lincoln's front porch. Claybrook had her morning paper under his arm and was holding a finger on the doorbell. The drapes covering the window were drawn. Except for the *ping, ping* of the bell sounding from its inside box the house was silent.

Wilma said, "Claybrook, if you want to live till

17

tomorrow you'd better take your finger off that bell."

"But she doesn't answer," argued Claybrook. "Where is she?"

"Probably," reasoned Wilma, "she's taking a bath, or maybe she's out back working in her plants."

"No," said Claybrook. "I already been to the back and looked. She's not there and everything's locked." He put his ear to the panel of the door and listened. "I don't hear any water running. Anyway, she wouldn't take a bath before she read her paper. Wilma?"

"Oh, for crack's sake," said Wilma, disgusted. "You wait here and I'll go around to the side and see if I can see in her bedroom. Will you wait here? I might could stand to be boiled in oil, but I don't know about you."

"I never heard of anybody being boiled in oil," said Claybrook. He waited on the porch only long enough for her to reach the double windows on the east side of the house and then came tearing around the corner of the building.

Built during the thrifty economy of a less prosperous time, Granny's house sat on a foundation of concrete block stilts and all of the windows were a good five feet from the ground. Now those to her bedroom were closed, as were the inside shutters covering them. And there was yet another hindrance to vision, the large live oak tree standing sentry just outside the panes. In full, lustrous leaf, some of its long evergreen branches had been lobbed so as to keep them from rubbing against the side of the building. The tree was one of Granny's sources of pleasure; to climb it was forbidden.

Standing beneath the tree, Claybrook said, "What we need is a ladder."

"I didn't think to bring one," said Wilma.

"Why don't we holler so she'll know we're out here?" Claybrook wanted to know.

"You holler," suggested Wilma. "This might be one of her days when she can stand you. She can never stand me."

"Grannnnny!" bellowed Claybrook. "Grannnnnny, it's us. Wilma and me! We're out here by your window. We were just passing by and thought we'd drop in for a second."

Nothing happened. There was no wind, and the garden, brilliant with bloom, was silent, so silent.

"She's in there but doesn't want to see us," reasoned Wilma. "Let's go."

A little war took place in Claybrook's face. He sniffed and dropped the newspaper. There came his decision. He rushed the tree, jumping from the ground to one of its limbs, and then swung himself up into its branches, monkey fashion. "Grannnnnny! Grannnnnny! You in there? It's me, Claybrook. Come to the window. I'm out here in your tree. Grannnnnny?" He had gained a height that was level with the windows. Skinny and lithe, holding fast to his branch, he leaned forward, peering. "I can see through the shutters just a little bit. I don't see Granny. She's not in bed."

"You'd better come down from there before you fall down," said Wilma. "Come on, let's go."

"There's a blanket on the floor," reported Claybrook. "And must be something under it. It just moved." He drew back, scowling, and then leaned forward again. "There. It moved again but I can't see what it is. What could it be? A dog?"

"Granny doesn't have a dog," said Wilma. "Claybrook, come down from there. Right now. *Right now,* you hear?"

Claybrook did not budge. His scream profaned the stillness. "Wilma, it's Granny under the blanket! She waved to me! She wants me! Wilma!"

"I hear you," she cried. "Crack's sake, give me a second."

"A rock!" roared Claybrook. "What we need is a rock. Find me one!"

Without pausing to examine this demand, Wilma ran first to one corner of the house and then to the other looking for a rock. There were none. She grabbed up a geranium growing in a heavy clay pot and with the strength of a rescuing fireman staggered back to the tree. The effort caused the muscles in her legs and arms to jerk and her heart to misbehave. Its sudden weight gain and the way it rocked and thumped made her gasp and wheeze.

His eyes gone as big as potatoes, Claybrook ogled her from his perch. "I told you a rock! That thing's no good. It's too heavy. Hurry up! Find me a rock!"

Her hat had slipped down over one eye and she had lost one of her six-shooters. She lowered the pot to the ground and looked toward Granny's greenhouse, a little homemade pillbox affair containing choice plants. A pile of half bricks was stacked against one of its screened sides. She ran to the structure, squatted, made her selection. She rose and turned but then turned back. Her mind cleared. She ran around to the back of the greenhouse and saw Granny's ladder lying in its usual place. As if it were a toy she snatched it up, hoisting it over her shoulder, and raced back to the tree. Claybrook was still screaming encouragement to the closed and shuttered windows. "We're coming, Granny, fast as we can!"

Panting, Wilma propped the end of the ladder against the window's ledge. She had never been good at climbing. Heights made her dizzy. Going up the ladder she made slits of her eyes. If she fell she didn't want to watch herself doing it. Cowardice in her drummed. Half to herself and half to Claybrook she muttered, "If I break this window for nothing, if Granny's not in there on the floor, they'll send us both to the prison farm."

"She's in there!" cried Claybrook. "She waved to me, I told you!"

Wilma said, "Turn around and pull the end of your branch up around you. I don't know what this glass is going to do." She pictured herself lying on the ground beneath the ladder, all bloody and with pieces of windowpane sticking up out of her chest. The windows were locked from the inside, she could see that.

She drew back her right hand, the one containing the half brick, and took aim. As if greased, the weapon went through the window, encountered the shutters. They parted and swung back. The glass, all but a little flying piece or two, fell to the floor inside. The sound of this crash did away with cowardice. "There," she said. "Now we can get inside and see what's what."

They found Granny on her bedroom floor. She had managed to pull a cotton blanket from her bed and under this wad lay wide-eyed. When Wilma and Claybrook bent over her she looked up at them, and to Claybrook, as if she might be commanding him to remove his hand from the jelly-bean jar, said, "Oh, stop that squalling and groaning. There's enough trouble here without that."

"Granny," said Wilma, "where are you hurt?"

"I don't know," answered Granny with something like shame. Her face, an older version of Wilma's, was dough white. "Two or three hours ago I got up and went to the bathroom, and when I came back in here I slipped and fell and every time I tried to stand up I fell again, so the last time I didn't try anymore. There's something wrong with my right leg. Maybe it's broken. What time is it?"

Wilma glanced at the clock on the bedside stand. It was lying on its side, the doily beneath it askew. A fringed throw rug was bunched against the foot posts of the bed. "It's nine-thirty. You want a drink of water?"

"No," said Granny. "I don't want any water. I'll just lie here till Doctor Bullock comes."

"Doctor Bullock is coming?"

"I want you to call him."

If a freight train ran over her she wouldn't take it any different, thought Wilma. On her haunches beside her grandmother, she said, "I think Dad should come. Or Mama. I think I'd better phone one of them."

"You go phone Doctor Bullock," said Granny.

"Tell him I can't come to his office. Tell him I want him to come immediately. I'll lie here till he gets here. Don't bother your father or mother with this. They'll know about it soon enough. Put my pillow under my head. What's that noise?"

"It's me," confessed Wilma, and tried to calm her breathing. There was an odd concentration in Granny's hard gaze, and this was making her nervous. There had never been any love lost between her and her grandmother.

She got the pillow from the bed and tucked it under Granny's head. When this was done she straightened the blanket covering her grandmother, fussing with it while trying to marshal her thoughts and make an independent decision. Independence was denied her. She had had too little practice with free-lance crisis decisions. All her life they had been made for her. So, taking Claybrook with her, she left the bedroom and went to the telephone table in the living room, found Doctor Bullock's number in the directory, and dialed it. After her conversation with the doctor Claybrook crept up to her and, whispering, wanted to know what he should do.

She said, "Claybrook, quit hanging on me. How should I know what you're supposed to do? Go wash something. The doctor will be here directly."

Claybrook made a trip to the kitchen and came back. "Everything's clean," he announced. And said, "You better call Dad or Mama."

"Granny told me not to," said Wilma. "You think I want to wake up dead tomorrow?"

"If you don't and something's bad off wrong with Granny you'll get it," said Claybrook. "Don't say I didn't tell you." He let himself out the front door and sat in the porch swing, watching the street. With every push of his feet the rusty chains supporting the suspended seat rattled and creaked.

Somebody ought to oil them, thought Wilma, and pulled her trousered legs up so that she sat in a jack-knife position on the hard little chair. After a minute she got up and went to the door of the bedroom and looked in. Granny appeared to be asleep.

She returned to the chair beside the telephone stand. A magazine on its lower shelf caught her eye and she grabbed this up and callously pawed through its sheets; it was secondhand, the kind to which her mother subscribed. Nothing in it but pictures of houses and furniture and long dull how-to pieces. Claybrook had left the porch, was washing the front walk with the hose. Across the street the waterless bay, the unplanned forest, shimmered dark green in the yellow sun.

She thought of her life in the woods, her private one shared with the soldiers of fortune and the international spy and all the others. Now, all of a sudden, it all seemed so far away. And unreal. She thought of her relationship with Granny, which had never been anything but a straw one. To Granny the comradeship of children was joyless. Her own son, Wilma's father, fell into this withered category.

Wilma sat unmoving in her chair until Doctor Bullock arrived. He was a stocky, countrified man with a round face and large, greedy ears who always made her think of the dark side of medicine: lepers, maniacs, dope fiends, things like that. Her parents and grandmother swore by his skill and knowledge, a sentiment she did not share. In her opinion he fell short of perfection. He knew the whole Lincoln family inside and out and seemed to think this gave him some kind of an edge. Once, in one of her younger years, she had been required to lie on his examining table bare naked while he thumped and probed for some hidden ailment. She had never forgiven him this vulgarity.

Now, lugging his physician's bag and followed by Claybrook, he came, all abluster. Never a one to waste time, with only a grunt for Wilma, he trotted past her as if he owned the house and entered Granny's bedroom, forgetting to close the door behind him. Even before he knelt beside the figure on the floor he had yanked his stethoscope from his bag.

Wilma got up to stand in the doorway to watch and listen. With his hand in her belt, Claybrook stood behind her and every second or so mustered the courage to peer around her.

As if she might be some kind of prize he had captured, Doctor Bullock moved from one side of Granny to the other on his knees, examining her with a bright, pleased expression, talking all the while. "Uh-huh uh-*huh*. Nice bruise here. Oh, and here's another one. But I don't think anything's busted. How you feel, Josie?"

"Dizzy," said Granny. "And sick to my stomach."

The doctor had taken a syringe and a bottle of

liquid from his bag, had pulled Granny's pajama trousers down from the waist and was swabbing a spot on her backside with a piece of moistened cotton. "You got no business living alone, Josie. I told you that the last time you was in my office for a checkup. What if them little grandchildren of yours hadn't just happened by? You could've laid here and died, do you know that?"

"Maybe that wouldn't have been a world tragedy," said Granny. "If you're going to stick me with that needle, do it."

With a quick, expert jab the doctor sunk his needle into the flesh of Granny's small rear. He sat back on his heels. "Now in just a minute you're going to start feeling sleepy-bye. Meanwhile, you and me have got a little decision to make. At the hospital we got east views and we got west ones. You tell me which you like best and I'll see to it you get it."

"I am not," said Granny, "going to the hospital."

Doctor Bullock laughed. "Oh, yes you are. We got to make some tests. I need me some pictures of what's going on inside you, and I sure can't bring the machinery to do it with here. How you feel now?"

"Better, I think," said Granny. "I hate hospitals."

"Now how do you know that?" said Doctor Bullock. "Unless you've been storying to me all these years you hadn't ever been confined to one."

"My husband died in your hospital," said Granny.

"He was sick," said Doctor Bullock in a tone laced with good humor and comfort. "You aren't. You're healthier than a plantation mule. I think all you got is a couple of little twisted wires. They're not anything can't be fixed, I don't think. You decide on what view you want yet?"

"If you're sure I've got to go," said Granny, "I'll take an east view. How am I going to get there?"

"Why," said the doctor, "I'm going to phone for an ambulance to come after you. And while we're waiting for it to get here I think I had just better phone Ted. He'll want in on this fun too."

"My son is not my keeper," said Granny, and closed her eyes. When the ambulance arrived and its two attendants put her on a stretcher and carried her from the house she only opened her eyes once to give them a look and then was asleep again.

The white vehicle decorated with its red crosses had no more than pulled away from the curbing in front of the house when Wilma's father came. The doctor met him at the door and hustled him out and down into the yard and the two stood talking. When their conversation was finished the doctor left and Wilma's father came into the house. He was a neat, dutiful man, the kind that could always be called on to be a last-minute pallbearer or distribute church baskets to the needy on Christmas Eve. As personnel manager for Timberlake's second largest sawmill he was a respected member of the community. His wife, Ida, mother to Wilma and Claybrook, was employed as a secretary in an insurance office.

Now, attempting to hide his nervousness and worry, Ted Lincoln addressed himself to his children. "Well, the excitement is over. I'll gather up what things

I think your granny will need while she's laid up and then close up here and get over to the hospital. You two had better go on home. There's nothing for you to hang around here for."

"I had to break the window in her bedroom so we could get in," said Wilma, shrewdly hurrying to offer her side of this matter before it was otherwise discovered. "Shouldn't we nail some boards over it or something?"

"I'll find something to cover it with until I can see to getting it fixed," said her father. He went through the house to the back porch, returning in a few minutes with some thumbtacks and a small sheet of clear plastic.

During her stay in the hospital only the parents went every evening to visit Granny. Ben Frost tended her plants and kept an eye on her house.

Some days later Wilma's parents brought Granny home. She now used a cane to help her get about and was testier than ever. Cannily observing, Wilma noticed some changes in her. There was a new, questioning brilliance in her eyes and there was a slight sag to the right side of her face. A housekeeper-companion had been hired to live with her, and for the homecoming occasion the woman had prepared a cold, attractive supper for all the Lincolns and herself. Granny kept the hired one hopping throughout the entire meal. At the end of three days the woman said to Wilma's parents, "I'm sorry for you people," and left.

There came another one who stuck it out for four

days. The third one, more hefty and determined than the first two, stayed a whole week. Craftily explaining this one's resignation, Granny said, "She whistled."

"She was cheerful," admitted Wilma's father.

"I can't stand people who are cheerful all the time," said Granny. "It's not natural."

"Well," said Wilma's father, "cheerful or uncheerful, I've run out of applicants for the job. There just aren't that many homeless women in Timberlake willing to go live in somebody else's house twenty-four hours a day. Not for what we can afford to pay."

"I can't afford to pay anything," observed Granny. "I showed you how much I have in my savings. And don't you and Ida offer me your charity again either. I won't have it. Why don't you all go home?"

"We'll go as soon as we get this settled," said Wilma's father. "It's not settled."

"It would be if you'd shut up talking about it," said Granny, pushing her hair forward and then backward and then stirring it into a messy tangle. She said, "I'm not your child, I'm your mother. Do you think I'm so barmy now I can't make my own decisions? What gives you the right to come in here telling me what to do?"

Said Ted Lincoln, showing some heat, "I'm your son, that's what gives it to me. I can't go home and leave you here by yourself."

"Why?"

"Because I can't. Because you can't live alone. Oh, I don't know what the answer to this is. You refuse to come live with us and you say you won't sell this place and go to the Timberlake Arms. So what am I supposed to do? Just walk off and forget you?"

"The Timberlake Arms," said Granny, huffy as an old pecked bird. "That place. All those little pigeonhole rooms. All those cackling freaks. They don't cackle so loud, I can tell you. They're afraid to. Peace is what you get at the Timberlake Arms. Lots of peace. They won't even let you have a cat in that place for company. They don't give their accommodations away either. This house is forty years old. Were I to sell it and move over there, how long do you think what I'd get for it would last? Just for a look-see Ben and I went over there one day. We found out what they charge. We saw what it was like. Well people and sick people all mixed up. It's not a retirement home and it's not a nursing home. It's a dump ground. No thanks, I'm all right here by myself. You all go home. I'll call you if I need you. Everybody go home."

Wilma's father threw up his hands. "Oh, the devil and branch water. Mother, you have got to understand. You've had an accident."

"That's true. An accident. Have you never had an accident?"

Dodging the question, Wilma's father produced a cramped smile. "You're seventy-nine years old. You'll be eighty your next birthday."

"You needn't remind me," said Granny. "I can still count."

"Mother, you made Doctor Bullock a promise."

"I know I did, but I've changed my mind about keeping it."

"Should I call him and tell him that?"

"Doctor Bullock is not my boss. He's my doctor."

"He's your friend and so am I. Between us I thought we had made you understand you can't live alone anymore."

"I understand it," said Granny. She turned sideways in her chair and made an ape's face.

"If you understand it," said Wilma's father, "tell me what you think we should do."

Granny was caught and she knew it. There was nothing to do but try for an honorable surrender. Her eyes went from face to face, searching. When her gaze reached Wilma it riveted. After some seconds had passed she said, "I won't allow another stranger in this house with me. But maybe Wilma could come stay until I'm well again. What would you say to that?"

Wilma, who had been sitting immobile and more or less disinterested during this whole exchange, jerked herself erect. She shuddered and a whole train of excuses went careening through her mind. They disappeared. Trying to recall one of them, she blinked and blinked again. Her relief was extreme when her father said, "Wilma has to go to school, Mother."

Said Granny, "Is she in school now?"

Wilma's mother decided to speak. She was a peace-loving, mild-mannered person whose own parents were still fairly youthful, safe and healthy on their farm in Mississippi. She said, "No, Mother Lincoln. Wilma is not in school now but will be come September. Meanwhile she has Claybrook to watch out after."

Almost at once Granny offered a countersolution. "She can watch out after Claybrook here as well as she can anywhere else. Can't she?"

Ted and Ida Lincoln swapped a look. They went outside and walked around, arms linked and heads bent close. Presently they invited Wilma to join them.

Barefooted and tousle-haired, she stood before them and, feeling herself trapped in their dilemma, said, "You decided."

They said, "No."

"You didn't? Then what'd you call me out here for?"

"To ask what you think."

"Me? I'm not supposed to be the one to say. You're supposed to tell me."

"No, Wilma. Not this time." Soft were their voices and their eyes sought nothing from her save recognition of the problem they were offering to share. There was no secure answer in their faces. They were looking at her as if she was *somebody*.

Unprepared, astonished, exposed, Wilma brought her hands up and laid them, one on top of the other, crosswise on the base of her throat. She felt the throb of her heart and it was strong and something else inside her was strong and willful and powerful. Of a sudden she felt ignorant of herself but buoyed up. Trying to hide whatever it was that was causing this, she scowled. "Well, I don't know what to say."

Her parents said, "Say what you think."

"Granny don't like me."

"True. That's her loss, but it's true."

"She don't like Claybrook either. I don't think we could get along with her."

With something like relief, her parents said, "All right. Then it's settled. The answer is no."

The power in her was a hard and steady beat. Drawing on its flattering worth and its mysterious ambition, she said, "I didn't say my answer was no. I only said she don't like us and I didn't think we could get along with her. I didn't mean we shouldn't try it. We got to do something, haven't we?"

So the problem was settled. For the remainder of the summer Wilma would live with Granny full time. Claybrook would be delivered to Granny's door every weekday morning at eight o'clock and collected at five P.M. The marketing and laundry would be done by Wilma's mother on Saturdays. On Sunday Wilma would come home and Granny would come with her. Sunday would be family day. Now. How did all this strike Granny?

On a beam of triumph Granny said, "Fine," and even allowed Claybrook to give her cheek a comforting pat.

"In the morning when we bring Claybrook we'll bring your clothes and your toothbrush and other things," said Wilma's mother. "Be sure all the doors are locked before you go to bed. Don't let anybody in unless you know who it is. And don't stay up past your regular bedtime."

"Yes," said Wilma. "All right." She followed her

parents and Claybrook out the front door and stood on the bottom front porch step until the street in front of Granny's house was once again black and empty. There was no light in any of Ben's windows. Night had come. In the darkened hammock across the way all of life had stolen to cover.

Wilma turned and went back into Granny's house and closed the door, remembering to shoot its bolt and fasten its lock chain.

Two

It was time, it was past time, for the relief of the summer rains. Still, they did not come. Without interference, with only some daily drifts of milk-white clouds for company, the sun over Timberlake was ruler. The days blazed and there was no coolness in the dawdling winds.

Granny's house was equipped with two window air-conditioning units. Years before, Wilma's parents had insisted on having these installed as a gift—a wasted piece of generosity. Every spring Wilma's father sent two men to take the units from their casings and clean and oil them, but there the attention to them ended. Granny would not allow their use. "It's not good for people to breathe artificial air," she said.

Claybrook said, "At home when it's hot as it is now we have ours on all the time and it don't hurt us."

"Your father and mother don't have to squeeze their every dollar," said Granny. "I do. I have to live on what those goose-brains up in Washington have figured out I can scratch by on. Would you happen to know what that means?"

Claybrook admitted he wouldn't. To him Washington wasn't even a mystery. He didn't know where it was or why it was so; it was nothing.

Granny was the mystery. No longer was she the familiar, forgivable figure always so much a part of Claybrook's past life. Someone else had stepped into her place, a little tyrant who picked at all his carefully designed jokes till he fell silent and sullen, who scorned his fear of house spiders and laughed at his revulsion of toad droppings that had to be washed each morning from the front and back walkways. Nothing he said or didn't say, nothing he did or didn't do, pleased this foreigner. From the time he arrived in the mornings until he left in the afternoons she was after him for first one thing and then another. Yet, because she was his granny and he had come by his sense of family loyalty by honest means, he declined to complain of the treatment being dished out to him. Further, he told Wilma that if she spoke of it to their parents he would say she was lying. "And they'll believe me because they know I always tell the truth." In this queer, ask-nothing devotion of his he was remote and obstinate, the most fragile form of innocence. He found, as he always had, his own simple pardons for Granny's behavior. "She don't mean it," he said. "She's old and some of her wires is twisted."

Into Granny's hostile brabble Wilma was also drawn. "It beats me," remarked Granny, "how a girl as big and old as you are can know so little how to go about the merest tasks."

"Housework has just never interested me much," said Wilma, unable to think of any other excuse for her worthless and slovenly being.

"Oh, I can tell that," said Granny. She had finished her tea-and-toast lunch, served by Wilma on a tray, and now sat in a chair by the front window thumbing through an old photograph album, holding a magnifying glass over the pictures, bending to examine the details in each. This research was not something that particularly interested her, it was merely something to do. She owned a television set, another unwanted gift, but what it showed her was useless. Worse than useless, it was mindless and tasteless. Its offerings insulted respectable human beings. Films about animals and nature and the goings-on in the nation were acceptable. Otherwise the box sat silent in its dark corner.

It was Wilma's third day with Granny. Early that morning the old one had had a quarrel with Ben Frost about the weeds that insisted on creeping from his yard over into hers. Ben said, "Josie, now you know I hadn't got any control over them weeds. They grow and I can't help it any more than you can. I'm an old man. I can't get out here and grub weeds in all this heat the way I used to."

"You could hire a gardener," said Granny, whacking at the weeds with her cane. "You can afford one. I can't."

Ben made a spiteful suggestion. "Josie, suppose you remove yourself from my property. You're standing on it and I don't like it. Go on. Back off and stay that way. I'm fed up with your yapping at me about these weeds. I'm tired of you. Back off now, I told you. You're sick, Josie. Go home and stay there."

In stunned disbelief Granny took several steps backward. After a long, frozen moment she said, "I am not sick, Ben. I have never felt better in my life."

Ben would say no more. He went across his yard to the utility house where he kept his gardening tools and came back with a hoe. Muttering to himself, he began attacking the trouble-making weeds.

Granny stumped back into her house and phoned the Timberlake animal shelter. She told her correspondent there that she was in the market for a large male dog, one that wouldn't cost her anything and would protect her and her property and be her companion. The kind she had in mind, she said, should not be vicious but would have to be resourceful because she was a widow living on government dole. What did dole mean? Well, a dole is a handout. But to get back to the matter of her dog. He should have some gumption. Be resourceful. There were rabbits and squirrels in the woods across the street from her house, and her dog could go there whenever he was hungry and forage for his food. Couldn't he?

The animal-shelter person didn't agree. Yes, it was the business of the shelter to find homes for lost or abandoned animals, and yes, they would keep Granny in mind in case a large, male, resourceful dog, one that was protective but not vicious, came in to them for placement, but surely there had to be another, better answer to Granny's present frail situation. In general dogs are dependent on their owners for food. They have to exercise every day but should not be allowed to run loose. Timberlake had a city ordinance against dogs' running loose. Dogs require regular veterinary care; they have to have periodic distemper and rabies shots. Some dogs have dental problems. Yes, they make good companions but they cannot take the place of a live human, even one who is only twelve, in the home of an older person just recovering from an accident. Was not the little granddaughter good to Granny? Had her neighbor actually threatened her? Should one of the senior citizens' groups be contacted? Possibly someone could be sent out to investigate.

Granny slammed the phone back in its cradle. "Of all the crust. You'd think being my age was some kind of disease, the way people talk to you."

"Some dogs slobber," commented Wilma. "And dig holes."

"It doesn't pay to be truthful anymore," ranted Granny. "I should have told that fancyprass I was twenty-five and ate steak every night for my supper with enough left over to feed eight dogs. He wanted to send somebody out here to investigate. Investigate what? I don't need investigating. He does. It's a good thing being dumb doesn't hurt. If it did, he'd scream all day."

"I made the beds and cleaned the bathroom," said Wilma. "Should I fix lunch now? Claybrook and me are going to have beef stew. It's all cooked. Mama brought it this morning. All I have to do is heat it."

"I'll have tea and toast," said Granny.

"Mama said you should eat some of her stew," argued Wilma. "It's got vegetables in it."

"I'll have tea and toast," repeated Granny. She almost lived on the parched bread and brown, sugared brew. What kept her going was a puzzle. Certainly it wasn't food.

Now it was early afternoon and the house was like a furnace. Claybrook was in the backyard building a bird feeder from some lumber scraps and other materials "borrowed" from Ben. Wilma was dusting the living room furniture, taking her own bored time with each piece. In a brushwood shelter in the woods across the street her playlike friends awaited her. She was their lieutenant and without her nothing could happen, so, huddled in the snow under their buffalo robes, they watched the ominous sky and waited. They would have a long wait. Their lieutenant was busy; she had this other, this wobbly and now not so heroic other.

As she knelt, red-faced and sweating, beside the table at Granny's elbow and passed her rag over its surface, Wilma chanced to look up and received a shock, for Granny, holding the photograph album on her lap, was bent forward watching her, and in the brilliant, intent eyes something disturbing glowed. What was it? Jealousy? Envy? A warning of some kind? What? And why?

Puzzled, helpless, aware, even a little alarmed, Wilma said, "Granny."

Whatever it was that had been in Granny's face fled. Of a sudden, deciding she wanted the longest conversation she and Wilma had ever had, she said, "You don't look a bit like your dad or your mama. Claybrook either."

"How I look don't bother me," said Wilma.

"Not that that's any kind of calamity, you understand," said Granny.

"The kinds of friends I've got don't care," said Wilma.

"Your hair is your only redeeming feature," said Granny, her face set as an old spiteful deacon's.

Stung, humiliated, Wilma ducked her head and passed her dustrag over her face. The same as always, there were the decades and decades between them, with their separating mists and differences, and, involved in this separation, their two languages, which had never really met except in spurts and jerks. There had been give and take sometimes in the way they used to talk to each other. But this now, this was something different. Vicious. A poison.

Wilma looked up and met Granny's ugly waiting gaze. Overlaid by caution, anger in her climbed. In a shudder of illumination she thought: She'd like me to jump up and paste her one so she could paste me back. Things have gone wrong with her so she wants them to go wrong with everybody else. She wants trouble. How awful to have only this left when you're seventy-nine. It's evil.

Evil. The word, so out of step with the everyday workings of her mind, hit her like a blow of a hammer. Appalled, feeling herself up against something shameful and guilty, Wilma was the first to give in, forcing herself to look away, to ignore, to take refuge in the safety of the unfinished dusting.

The silence and heat in the room were suffocating. There was Granny's defeated sigh, and then again she turned her attention to the photograph album. Presently, in a normal tone, she said, "You want to see a picture of me when I was your age?" She placed the album on the table between herself and Wilma and pointed. "There. That was me."

Wilma gazed at the sepia-colored photo pasted to the black page. It showed her a stout, fierce-faced, rakish-looking young female outfitted in a fur-trimmed coat that hit her legs mid-calf. Her dark hair fell from its center part to her waist in disarray. Hardly a picture of sweet girlhood, she looked ready to spring at the unseen photo taker.

Humoring her, Wilma said, "You were only twelve when this picture was taken?"

"I was grown by the time I was twelve," said Granny. "I had to be. My mother died when I was three and then my father took on my raising. He didn't waste any time doing it either."

"What kind of work did he do?"

"He was a telegraph operator by trade but only

worked at it when the spirit moved him. He had more important things on his mind. He liked causes. You might say he was a professional cause chaser. Show him a cause and he'd park me with whichever of his friends happened to be handiest at the time and run off and get mixed up in it. He liked Indians and went to a lot of trouble learning some of their dialects so he could get up in court and interpret for them. The Indians in South Dakota weren't having such an easy time of it back in those days. The white devils had pushed them off their land, and every once in a while they'd think about it and start another ruckus. They were always in court trying to make themselves understood. Fat lot of good it did them."

"You lived in South Dakota when you were young?"

"I was born there."

"I didn't know that."

"I expect there are a lot of things you don't know."

"Did you ever tell me any of this stuff before?"

"I might have when you were a baby. Your folks used to bring you over here and dump you on me every time they wanted to go gallivanting."

"When your father would park you with one of his friends and run off to see about one of his causes did you go to school?"

"Sometimes, but mostly not. It wasn't till I got married that I learned anything much beyond the three R's. My husband was an educated man; he taught me and I remember how mad he used to get at my ignorance. My father's friends weren't what you would call

school-minded. Those I remember clearest were enter-
tainers—singers, comedians, dancers, actors, people
like that. One time I lived with a couple named Borden
and Rosa Hall. They owned an old bug-trap hotel
named The Tin Horn, where all the gold hunters and
hay shakers and other lads used to come on Saturday
nights to do their fighting and gambling and drinking.
I forget what town that was in. One night Borden got
himself killed by some smart-talking cutthroat from
Wyoming named Hot Money Smith."

"Why?"

"Why what?"

"Why was his name Hot Money?"

"I don't think anybody got around to asking him
that. After he shot Borden they took him outside and
hung him. Rosa wouldn't let me look. Then they came
back in and took up a collection for Borden's funeral.
It was right nice. They don't make them like Borden
anymore. He and Rosa wanted to adopt me but could
never get my father settled down long enough to talk
to them about it. He had a funny nickname for me.
He called me Uncle Buck, and Borden didn't like it.
He thought it was disgraceful."

"You were your father's uncle?"

"Of course not. How could I be my father's uncle?
I was his child. He only called me Uncle Buck as a
joke. To make people laugh. Borden's nickname for
me was Queen of Hearts."

"The queen of hearts is always the loser," said
Wilma.

"What?"

"In the game of hearts. The card game."

"I know nothing about cards," said Granny. "It never made any sense to me to see a bunch of grown men sitting around gnashing their teeth over some silly pieces of cardboard. After Borden was killed Rosa bought me some fancy duds and taught me how to sing."

"Sing what?"

"Songs. Nice, pretty ones. No *boom, pah-pah*. My songs were all about the lonesome prairie and mothers and home. They were brawl stoppers."

"What're brawl stoppers?"

"The men who came to The Tin Horn to fight and gamble would forget what they had come for when I'd get up on a table and start one of my songs. It would be so quiet you could hear a pin drop. Everybody would cry. Rosa had a head for business. She was a looker too. I always wished my father would have married her. She would have made him a good wife. He mightn't have made her a good husband, though, so maybe it's just as well they never got around to looking at each other except as friends."

"I bet I would have liked your father," said Wilma. "I think it's funny my dad never told me anything about him."

"He was a corker," said Granny. "He and your father only met once or twice. They didn't exactly gee and haw."

"What's gee and haw?"

"They didn't hit it off. Your dad was a little sober britches and didn't like scary tales. I never had to teach him how to work and save his money, though. Your great-grandpa never cared anything about money except when he didn't have any. One time he and I lived in a tent and washed our clothes and dishes and ourselves in Canoe Creek. What state that was in escapes me. We were always traveling. Your great-grandpa wasn't a saintly man, but when he thought to remember he was one he was a good father. The Wild West wasn't made for people like your dad. He's never liked to have me tell about the way I grew up so I never talk about it much."

"Oh," breathed Wilma, having been raised for a few minutes into a world far more interesting and brighter than her own. "I wish I could have been alive back in those days." She craved to hear more about Borden and Rosa Hall and their bug-trap hotel and Canoe Creek and the great-grandpa chasing lickety-cut all over the raw and drastic West after his causes. And the young Josie Lincoln standing on a table in The Tin Horn singing her songs. Enriched, transfixed, aroused, thirsting for more, afraid to ask for more, wanting to give something more of herself than was required, she said, "You know what? I just thought of a way you and I could pass the time when we haven't got anything else to do. We could sing songs."

Said Granny, "Oh, that's a dandy idea."

"You don't like it?"

"It doesn't thrill me. I'm too old for songs."

"I don't see how that is."

"Of course you don't. You're twelve, so you don't

see how a lot of things are. You're like Old Dobbin."

"Who's Old Dobbin?"

"He was a horse in a song I used to sing. It didn't say so but I always had the feeling he was wearing blinders. Drawing his shay through fields of clover on their golden wedding day."

"Whose golden wedding day?"

"Whosever golden wedding day it was. The song didn't name any names. What do you think of somebody my age? What do you think of me being seventy-nine, almost eighty?"

"I don't see anything wrong with it."

"What do you think the difference between you and me is?"

"I don't know. I'm twelve and you're seventy-nine. . . ."

"Is that all?"

"You're old."

"You think being seventy-nine is a sin?"

"You didn't do it."

"No," agreed Granny without any sadness or self-pity or anything else in her tone except recognition of the truth. "I didn't do it." She lifted the photograph album from the table, set it on her lap, put her head back against the headrest of her chair, closed her eyes, and presently slept. Every afternoon it was the same. Sleep, sleep. Then the little flurry of Claybrook's five-o'clock departure involving a few get-away words with one of the tired parents, then the unwanted supper, a slow walk around the house to inspect the plants growing in their tubs and pots and cans, a television program if a suitable one was available, then darkness and more sleep.

Creeping around the room in her bare feet, Wilma finished her dusting, pausing every now and then to glance at the unconscious figure sprawled in the over-stuffed chair. In her sleep, the vitality in her withdrawn and still, Granny was an unlovely sight. There were the slack mouth and the thin crinkled skin. The stiff white hair was yellowed in spots. Every line of her sagged. Here was decay, ruthless, forsaken, and terrible, without consolation. Why was this? Why did it have to be?

God, thought Wilma, must hate people to make them go through this awful business. Repulsed and experiencing within herself an ugly, shameful failure of some kind that whispered of wrong, she turned away, but then a sound coming from Granny made her turn back. It was a low, slow sigh that rose, trembling, to surrender to a moan that struggled for existence. Suffering, on a note of fear, it rose and fell. It was the most terrible sound Wilma had ever heard.

It stopped. Within its grip, stunned, afraid, Wilma made herself move. She leaned over the still form. She put her hand over the still face and felt the escaping breath.

In her sleep Granny shifted her position and was quiet, and at length Wilma turned away. In the solitude of her own room she stood before a full-length mirror, staring at herself. Wondering, caught up in a circle of questions, she stood there a long time.

Three

Claybrook's bird feeder was no carpenter's dream fulfilled. It was a one-man two-day project over which he huffed and puffed and once, in a frenzy of frustration, even screamed. When, finally, the box was finished, he brought it inside and set it down in front of Granny. He was filthy. He sported a swollen black-and-blue thumb, a limp, and some dried blood. His eyes shone. Proffering his present, he said, "If you'll let me, I can get a piece of wire and hang it up in the tree outside your bedroom window. Then when the birds come to eat you can watch them."

Granny lowered her newspaper, adjusted her glasses, and leaned forward, peering. She discovered a major flaw. "But you didn't leave them any place to perch," she said. "They have to have somewhere to sit while they feed, and you haven't left them anything."

Claybrook's joy in his masterpiece vanished. Dismally he eyed the now imperfect feeder. He sought a solution to his grave problem. Turning the box so that Granny could better view one of its more fortunate qualities, he said, "They can go inside when they want to eat. See? I made them a door."

"I see," said Granny.

"But maybe I should've left them a place to stand on so if they wanted to stay outside and eat they could do that too," said Claybrook. His eyes lighted. "I know how I can fix it. I can take this back outside and nail it to a board. Then the birds would have a perch, wouldn't they?"

"I suppose they would," said Granny. It was a Friday, Wilma's and Claybrook's first with her, and she had spent a large part of it ransacking drawers, cabinets, and closets looking for something lost but cannily refusing to name the object or objects of her unsuccessful search.

Next door Ben had been busy. Four landscapers had arrived shortly after sunrise that morning in a flatbed truck loaded with full-grown bushes, and by two o'clock between Ben's house and Granny's there was an expensive, thickset, made-to-order green-and-yellow living screen six feet high. Not once during the whole of this activity did Granny acknowledge it. To Wilma she observed that the kitchen floor and all the windows and their sills needed a good cleaning and suggested that this work be done in a spirit of willingness and cheer.

Now it was close to four o'clock, and for a change Granny was wide awake in her chair. Finished with her criticism of Claybrook's bird feeder, she was ready to discuss a more important subject. In the way of an angry orchestral conductor rapping his musicians to attention she launched it by whacking twice at the legs of the nearest table with the tip of her cane. She made a sharp, emphatic announcement. "I had two gold pieces," she said. "But now it seems I don't have them anymore. They're gone."

Holding his bird feeder, Claybrook rose. He stood motionless. With sincerity, and on a high note of honest curiosity, he said, "Where'd they go?"

"I always kept them in my handkerchief box," said Granny. "They were there yesterday. Today they aren't."

"What'd they look like?" asked Wilma, uncaring and languid. In her make-believe life, the one played with her fictional friends in the woods, gold in one form or another was something she frequently risked life and limb for. Several times she had died for it, but she had never actually seen a piece of the precious metal, especially any gold coins. All that day she had toiled, and now, tired and hot and smelly, she sat on the floor with her knees drawn up to her chin and her back up against the open front door looking out through the separating screen at the empty street and what lay on its opposite side. Her hands were water-puckered, her shoulders and arms pained her. Over there in the bushes, the green bushes, gloomy and sweet and cool, was where she longed to be. She turned her head and trained a glazed look on Granny. "I say, what'd they look like?"

"One was a five-dollar piece and the other was a twenty," said Granny.

"I haven't seen them," said Wilma.

"I didn't either," said Claybrook.

"Well," said Granny, "they're gone. I know they couldn't have sprouted legs and walked off by themselves."

This piece of wit delighted Claybrook. "No," he agreed. "They couldn't have done that." A grin that invited Granny's participation spread across his face.

"This is no grinning matter," said Granny. Her tone accused, and through it ran a stout line of threat. "If you think it is, wait till your father gets here. Then maybe you'll grin on the other side of your face."

In Wilma shocked realization flooded. She stood and walked toward Claybrook. She put her arm around her brother's shoulders and awkwardly drew him to her. "Claybrook, let's go outside and sit in the swing until Dad comes."

Claybrook looked up at her. "What's wrong?"

"Nothing. I just want us to go outside and wait for Dad. It won't be but a few minutes."

"I don't want to. It's too hot out there. Besides, I need to find me a piece of wire."

"You don't need any wire now, Claybrook. Come on, let's go out on the porch and wait for Dad."

Sensing something amiss, Claybrook sobered his

face. He licked sweat drops from his upper lip and rubbed his eyes with his balled fists. There was a silence and then he said, "What about the gold pieces? If they're lost, we ought to help find them."

"Clay," said Wilma, "*please* shut up your face. *Please* come with me." She felt emptied and, in some senseless, despairing way, beyond the reaches of her understanding, lonely and painfully altered. She avoided looking at the old one who had had her say, who had hung the crooked head of her cane over the arm of her chair and taken up her paper, holding it like a shield in front of her face.

The father was later than usual in coming. He had brought a Chinese supper for two. When he came up onto the porch and saw Claybrook and Wilma sitting in the swing, Claybrook's bird feeder between them, he stopped and shifted his parcels from one arm to the other. He wore his Friday, thank-the-Lord look. To Claybrook he said, "You look wrung out, son. You shouldn't go at things so hard, especially in all this heat. You get your feeder finished?"

Claybrook had had time to figure out the unpleasant business concerning the gold pieces. He had done this unaided and in rigid, miserable silence, and now the ugly truth of it put an end to his past rules and standards. His honesty and loyalty had been spit upon and he was ready to spit back. He trained his eyes on the father and in a wrathful fury said, "Yeah, it's finished and I hate it. I hate her and after today I'm not ever coming back here."

"You hate who?" said the father.

"Her!" howled Claybrook, abandoning calm. "Granny! She thinks I stole her gold pieces. I didn't. I didn't even know she had any. I never even go in her room except when I help Wilma clean in there." He snatched his bird feeder up and pitched it out across the porch railing. It landed on its side in the grass; its little fragile door slowly swung open, hanging askew. The father watched this act of destruction and then he came across to the swing and set his two paper bags containing the Chinese food down between Wilma and Claybrook. From one he withdrew a carton containing plump fried shrimps, still warm. He handed it to Wilma. "Here. You and Claybrook eat these. They'll make you feel better."

"I don't want any," shrieked Claybrook. "I want to go home." He jumped from the swing and ran across the porch and down the steps and walkway to the car parked at the curb. He yanked at the door and as soon as it opened dived in, slamming it behind him. He slid down in the seat so that not even the top of his head showed.

"Oh," said the father in a tone of loss, "oh, I wish this needn't have happened."

Wilma picked one of the largest shrimps from the carton and stuffed the whole thing into her mouth. She didn't want to have to explain anything or help make any decision. She had a hard time swallowing the shrimp. One way or another it will have to be changed now, she thought, and I don't want to be blamed if how it's changed is wrong. I'm just a little kid. I'm not supposed to go around telling people what to do. They're supposed to tell me. She saw her father's fatigue and anxiety and isolation and sought from her own intelligence some offering, some comfort. She found nothing save a wallowing shred. "It wasn't just the gold pieces," she said. "It was everything, but he wouldn't let me tell you. If she had some gold pieces, they're still in the house somewhere. She said herself they couldn't have just sprouted legs and walked off." She wanted, almost more than she had ever wanted anything, to hear her father order her to join Claybrook in the car, but this didn't happen. He left her and the Chinese supper in the swing and went inside to find Granny, who had retreated to her bedroom. In twenty minutes he was back with a terse report. "We found the gold pieces. They were right where she hid them, in the toe of her good shoes."

Because he looked so alone, so tired, so as if he needed something to lean on, because he was her father and she had never given him much of anything of herself beyond simple obedience and modest affection, she wanted to give him a present. Not anything like an IOU (one penniless Father's Day she had given him one of those) or socks or a can of his favorite shaving foam, not anything like that, but something important that would be remembered. But she had nothing important to give, so, drawing from a reckless heroic, she delivered the next best thing, saying, "Well, Granny's old and forgets things. It's not her fault. Probably after a while she'll tell me she's sorry, but what're we going to do about Claybrook?" Aware that she had given her gift but aware also that she had gone too far with it, had crossed a threshold of some kind into a realm new to her, she put her lips together.

She watched her father swallow. He loosened his tie. He turned away and turned back. In a rich, strange tone there came his answer. "I'll have to talk to your mother about Clay." He came over to the swing and helped himself to one of the shrimps. "These any good?"

"Yes," answered Wilma, making her mouth and eyes behave, "they're good." Her father leaned and smoothed her eyebrows with his thumb and then went down into the yard and retrieved the bird feeder. Carrying it, he walked to the car, opened the back door, and set it inside. Then he went around and got in and drove off, remembering to turn and wave a temporary good-bye. Responding, she watched her arm shoot up into the air as if it didn't belong to her. "'Bye! Don't forget to come get us Sunday! That's family day, don't forget!" The car reached the end of the street, paused for the stop sign, turned, and was lost to vision.

Darkness was still hours away. Showing through the trees on the other side of the street, the lowering sun still shone yellow, but the air had begun to stir and cool and on the far horizon beyond the trees there began to swell a mass of smoke-colored clouds. Rain was coming.

Feeling herself trapped and lost and unheroic, dreading the evening meal, Wilma gathered up the bags containing the Chinese food and the half-emptied carton of shrimps and went inside the house to the kitchen. She heated everything except the fortune cookies, laid places for two at the kitchen table, and then went to the door of Granny's room. It was closed but not locked. During Granny's stay in the hospital all the inside locks in the house had been removed from their doors. Wilma rapped.

Silence.

She put her hand on the doorknob and pushed. There was something on the other side, a barrier of some kind. The panel only opened an inch. Wilma spoke to the crack. "Granny, I've got supper ready. Come on out and let's eat."

The voice on the other side of the door was so close and harsh it made her jump. "I don't want any supper. Get away from this door."

"It's Chinese. Dad brought it from town."

"I don't want anything Chinese. I'm an American."

"Granny, this is good food. I tasted it."

"If you like it you eat it. Eat it all." The crack in the door disappeared. Wilma was left standing in the cramped, dark hall staring at blank wood. Her heart began to beat unnaturally fast. Anger such as she had never known took hold of her. Grimly she looked around for a weapon. Her eyes lit on a tightly rolled umbrella standing upright in a corner. She leaped for it, seized it, and returned to the closed door. She took a fencer's stance, and, as if the door were alive and she could make it perform, began to jump at it and jab it with the point of the umbrella, but then, getting down to more serious business, began to whack at the panel with serious, vicious strokes. "You! Come on outa there! I say come outa there right this minute!

What do you think this is anyway? You think just because you're old and had an accident you can treat people just any old way? You've run Claybrook off, you want me to go too? I will! I'll go! And then where will you be?"

Nothing happened. The door did not open. On the other side of it Granny remained silent.

"All right!" shrilled Wilma, whacking away. "Stay in there and starve! See if I care. See if anybody cares. Stay in there and rot. You and your old gold pieces. You knew where they were all the time, you knew we didn't steal them from you, you just said that to make trouble. Okay, you wanted trouble and now you've got some! I'm going, Granny, and then you'll be all by yourself. I'll give you till I count to three to come outa there and behave yourself. Are you listening? One!" *Whack.* "Two!" *Whack.* "Three!" *Whack.*

Silence.

The umbrella had taken all the punishment it could stand. The cloth part of it was hanging from its spokes in tatters, its staff was broken. Wilma threw the pieces of it at the door, whirled, ran to her room, yanked her hat and her belt containing her six-shooters from the bottom drawer of her bureau, and quit the house. She sped across the street and entered the woods, running zigzag through the trees, dodging thorny underbrush thickets, searching for her friends, once even foolishly calling out to them as if they were real live people.

They were gone, all gone. Their camp was deserted, they had left no sign for her, not even a feather or a farewell rock message. Stunned, unable to summon anything from her imagination, which never before had failed her, she lay down on a patch of slick dried pine needles, propping herself on her elbows. She put her head back and the tears rolled from her eyes down the corners and into her ears. Something had happened. It was finished, that other life of hers. Something had taken its magic from her, and now, surrendering to the loss of it, to something larger, to reality, she wept.

Chased by the westerly winds, the clouds had moved over until they hung directly above her. The rain started.

It was dark before she emerged from the woods and went back across the street to Granny's house. A single light showed through the dark, glistening windows. The door was locked; she had to ring the bell and identify herself before Granny let her in. The old one wanted to know where she had been.

"Nowhere," said Wilma.

"It's raining," said Granny, returning to her chair.

"I didn't notice," said Wilma.

"I ate my supper."

"Good for you."

"And I washed the dishes."

"You shouldn't have. That's my job."

"I didn't," said Granny in a strangely spent voice, "know if you were coming back."

"I came back because I had to," said Wilma. "Because there's nobody else."

Granny took a handkerchief from her apron pocket

and spread it on her knee, smoothing it, folding it, unfolding it, smoothing. "That young man was back."

"What young man?"

"The one who rides his motorcycle up and down this street."

"Well, this street doesn't belong to you."

"No, but my lawn does. He came right up onto my lawn. Tomorrow you'll see what he did to it. I was standing on the walk looking for you and he went around me and around me. I tried to get back up the steps but he wouldn't let me. He just screamed and laughed and kept going around making that machine of his rear up like a horse. The sparks just flew from his machine. I couldn't move, all I could do was just stand there. I don't know what he was trying to do, maybe kill me. He's crazy and ought to be locked up."

"Did you call the police?"

"No."

"Why not?"

"I wasn't thinking right. After he quit and left I came back on in the house and phoned Ben. I thought he might do something but he wouldn't talk to me. He hung up. He's still mad at me. Maybe this time he'll stay that way."

"Maybe he will," agreed Wilma. Her wet clothes were cold against her skin. She wanted to go to her room and put on pajamas and climb into bed and forget everything, but she continued to stand there looking at her grandmother.

Granny put her hands to her hair, pushing it forward and then backward and then stirring it. After a minute, accompanied by the beating of the rain on the roof, she made her strained apology. "It is a terrible thing," she said, "for a person like me to have enough sense left to know when I am being mean and childish and unreasonable and still not be able to stop."

The impact of these words, their meaning, all the unspoken things in them, did not hit Wilma until an hour later when, padding around the house in her pajamas, checking all the door locks and window latches, she passed the table beside Granny's empty chair. Intending to discard the newspaper lying on it, she picked it up and saw then the plumber's wrench lying there. Puzzled, she leaned and lifted the tool and held it in both hands. She heard the rain and the wind swooshing over and around the house and there began to seep into her consciousness a slow, enslaving truth. Granny was afraid. Of someone who might come in the night to rob and harm her, of people in the street, of living, of dying, of herself, of having now to depend on others to tell her what to do, of trying to make some sense out of a world she could not flee until that too was decided for her, Granny was afraid.

Astounded at the force of these rootless revelations, so strange, so beyond experience, Wilma went around and sat down in the grandmother's chair. She laid the wrench in her lap and covered it with her hands. Where, she thought, are the answers for people like her? The remedies? Where?

Four

Sometime during the night the rain stopped. By Saturday morning there was nothing left of Friday's late tempest save a few paled, northbound clouds.

After their breakfast Wilma and Granny went outside to view the damage left by the cowboy cyclist of the night before. On the front lawn there were long swaths of deep burn marks that the rain had not erased. There were clumps of uprooted grass and a string of churned holes. Sickened, feeling her whole world of right and wrong in some kind of danger, under some kind of attack, Wilma stood with her knuckles to her mouth, staring at this destruction. Here was no mere kid mischief. Here was not only wickedness but malicious and brutish wickedness. The sun was out and the air was light and scented.

Kneeling beside one of the holes, poking around in it with the tip of her cane, withdrawing crushed and mangled roots from it, Granny seemed to have shrunk. The expression on her face was strangely crippled, and when she spoke her voice seemed unable to decide whether it should be regretful or indignant. "Well," she said, "this just proves to me what I've been thinking for a long time now. Man is just as mean and bad and ugly as the day our Creator put him here. Just as wild and cussed."

"What man?" said Wilma.

"Man," said Granny. "Mankind. People."

"I think we ought to call the police," said Wilma. "They'll know who did this. It's the same one ran into that little car out there in the street just before you had your accident, so they know his name. You want me to go inside and call them?"

Temptation, then doubt, then decision swept across Granny's face. "No," she said. "They wouldn't do anything. It would only be my word against that lunatic's. Anyway, I don't want any trouble, so we'll just handle this ourselves. Go around to the back, Wilma, and find my rake and shovel. Drag the hose around here too. If we hurry I think we can fix this before your mother gets here with the groceries. I don't want her or your dad to know about this."

"If it was me," argued Wilma darkly, "I'd fix that jerk. I'd get me a big stick of dynamite and the next time he showed his face around here I'd let him have it. *Booooom!* No more jerk, no more motorcycle."

To this suggestion Granny made no reply. She had lowered herself to a sitting position on the ground, her feet stuck out in front of her in a child's attitude. Ben's new hedge sparkled in the sun. Through its green and yellow foliage Wilma could see the neighbor sitting in his rocker on his front porch. Complete to ten-gallon hat and pointed-toed boots, he was rigged out in one of his ranch-owner outfits and was being coyly uncurious about what was taking place next door. He was playing one of his ranch games, pretending his rocker was his horse and he was rounding up cattle. *"Hiyeeeeee! Git along there, little dogie!"* With the coiled rope in his hands he lassoed a bush growing near his porch steps, and reared back in his chair, grinning. *"Hiyeeeeee! Gotcha!"*

Batty old cockroach, thought Wilma, loping around to the back of Granny's house for the tools and hose. Within the hour the repair to the lawn, under Granny's supervision, was completed. There was some leftover dirt and Wilma sprayed it with water until it disappeared into the earth between the bruised grass runners. "Now," said Granny, "if your mother notices any of this when she comes what I'll do is tell her a mole did it."

For her part Wilma wanted none of this white lie—not because it offended her sense of right but rather because she longed for justice to be done, and this cover-up of Granny's wasn't it.

Returning the hose and rake and shovel to the backyard, she drew several pictures in her mind of how, if it were left up to her, the scales could be balanced. The Jerk could be staked out, stark naked, on the Sahara, or even that desert in Arizona, and be given no water to drink and no food for fourteen days. No, it would be better to leave him with a bucket of water, but it should be hung high in a tree where he couldn't get to it. Put a teeny hole in the bottom of the pail so he could watch its slow drip, drip while he dried and fried. While ants and lizards crawled around on him, tasting him. Since he was a jerk and therefore ignorant he wouldn't be able to speak the language of Arabs, so even if some came by and stopped he wouldn't be able to make them understand that he wasn't out there by choice. So they'd think he was taking a cure for a lung disease or something like that. So they'd get back on their horses and ride away. At night the jackals and coyotes would come and sit around him in a circle, snarling and howling. At the end of the fourteen days, if he was still alive, he'd think twice before deciding to scare any more old helpless ladies. Tearing around on his crazy old motorcycle ripping up their lawns.

Following this version of revenge there came another. In this one the Jerk was confronted, in a walled canyon, by a boa constrictor, and the Jerk couldn't get past or around the beast and make a run for his motorcycle because every time he moved so did the boa. In fact, the boa thought the motorcycle was a living enemy, so he wrapped his long, strong body around it and slowly crushed it to a pulp. A group of tourists on donkeys came riding along the rim of the canyon about this time and they dismounted and looked down just in time to see the Jerk's flailing feet disappearing into the boa's huge mouth. Said one of them, "That must be a mean snake." And said another, "I think you're right, but since we're riding donkeys, not motorcycles, I don't believe he'll bother us. Probably that jerk he just swallowed was trespassing on his property. Snakes aren't much different from people. Just like us, their homes are their castles. This looks like a nice lunch spot. Let's eat."

There were weak spots in both these avenging fantasies, but before Wilma had time to go back and improve any of their details her mother arrived with two bags of groceries. With her there came a woman who was identified to Wilma and Granny as a childhood friend of Wilma's mother. She had a cupid's face and her butter-yellow hair was magnificently piled. Her name was Azella Screechfield and she and her husband had only arrived the day before. They were in Timberlake seeking a new and better life. Mr. Screechfield and Wilma's father were, right this minute, out scouting around looking at job possibilities.

"Screechfield," said Granny. "A long time ago I knew another person with that name. It's been years since I thought about him. That was when I was a young girl out West. Maybe you and he are related."

"Oh, no, Grandma," said Mrs. Screechfield as if Granny didn't have a name and as if it were impossible for anybody by the name of Screechfield to be from anywhere but Mississippi. "My husband's people were all born and reared in the South. So were mine. I was a Davis before I married into the Screechfields."

"Well," said Granny, "West or South, we're all of

the same skillet." She excused herself and went to her bedroom and was gone for about ten minutes. When she returned to the living room she carried two knitting needles, a ball of tan yarn, and an immense knitted garment of the same shade, which appeared to be unfinished. Its body, thick here and thin there, was safety-pinned to two tube-shaped sleeves. The washing machine on the back porch was chugging away full force and Wilma's mother was in the kitchen putting the groceries away. She had declined offers of assistance from Wilma and Mrs. Screechfield, saying she could get her jobs done faster if allowed to work alone.

The visitor from Mississippi had seated herself beside Wilma on the sofa and was watching Granny, who had plopped herself down in her chair and was smiling at the knitted wad in her lap.

Never before in her life had Wilma seen her grandmother knit or, for that matter, even sew on a button or mend a tear. In this respect they were alike, she and Granny. If pins or gummed tape couldn't do the trick, then to heck with it.

Covertly Wilma studied Mrs. Screechfield's hair. It was beautiful except that its crown of fluffy little buns and curls didn't quite match the rest of it. The side tendrils and back upsweep had root streaks of a darker and duller shade than the topknot.

I bet the top's not real, thought Wilma, and with the broad end of a toothpick began removing the dirt from beneath her fingernails, wiping the gleanings on the cuffs of her shorts. Mrs. Screechfield's voice had the soft, honeysuckle quality of the true deep-Souther's. "I see you knit," she said, addressing herself to Granny.

"Oh, yes," said Granny, caressing the garment as if it was something precious and sacred. She lifted it and looked at it as she would have looked at an old loved friend. "I love any kind of needlework. The only trouble is, my eyes aren't what they used to be. I keep thinking I ought to go and have my glasses changed. Uh-oh. I do believe that's a dropped stitch. Or is it? Rats. I can't tell."

"Can I help?" said Mrs. Screechfield, half rising. "I have a great-aunt who knits."

"No, no," protested Granny, and stretched her mouth until a senseless smile appeared. "It's Wilma's job to straighten me out when I get confused like this. If you will, you just sit there and keep me company till Ida gets through back there. It isn't often I get to visit with anybody except the members of my immediate family. I need news from the outside world. You know, I could do my own laundry except Ida and Ted think I shouldn't since I had my accident."

She needs news from the outside world like a submarine needs a screen door, thought Wilma. She gets an hour of it every night on television and sees it all in the paper every day and don't like any of it. Wondering what kind of act this was, she heaved herself from the sofa, went to Granny's chair, knelt beside it, and took up the sweater or coat, or whatever the garment was, in both hands. The smell of mothballs and old dust assailed her nostrils. Suffering cats, she thought.

This rag must be a hundred years old; not even a freezing dog would be caught dead in it. She couldn't locate anything that looked like a dropped stitch to her. "Here," she said, returning the garment to Granny's hands. "You're okay. It's all the same."

From there on the show got better. After the fashion of a zealous teacher instructing a backward, after-hours student, Mrs. Screechfield commenced to talk of the outside world, and Granny, as if she had never set foot outside Timberlake or heard of anything more recent than the War Between the States, produced a child's wondering expression and from time to time made rambling contributions to the conversation. Occasionally she'd let out a little shriek and roll her eyes upward. The shrieks startled the visitor, but at the same time seemed to satisfy her. She spoke of the crime and violence in the cities and of all the new scientific things coming to light: wonder medicines, the control of population growth, and the new methods of education. Motels had replaced hotels, she said, and pretty soon everybody would be living in a high-rise apartment or condominium. Granny wanted to know what a condominium was, and Mrs. Screechfield explained. Granny said she didn't think she would care to live in a place where she couldn't have a clothesline. She said she herself was just a plain old dirt farmer, or would be if she owned enough land to go along with her ambitions and could be fifty again. Said if her own heart gave out before the rest of her did she didn't want any doctor pawing around in her chest trying to foist somebody else's organs on her even if it meant she would live to be a hundred. Said she preferred a living garbage man, one she could talk to on Tuesdays and Fridays, to a hole in the sink. Not that the man who collected her garbage on Tuesdays and Fridays was all that friendly.

Mrs. Screechfield turned her attention to matters of a more personal nature. She said she and her husband had made good time driving to Timberlake from Mississippi in their Chrysler. It was not a new model but it was faithful.

Granny said, "My husband and I owned a Pilgrim once."

"A Pilgrim what?" said Mrs. Screechfield.

"Automobile," said Granny.

"I never heard of that make," said Mrs. Screechfield.

"Well," said Granny, "we had one. It was made in Detroit and was dark blue. On second thought maybe it wasn't a Pilgrim. Maybe it was a Plymouth. I always get Pilgrims and Plymouths mixed up. As I remember my history the Pilgrims landed at Plymouth Rock. Didn't they?"

"Yes," said Mrs. Screechfield gently, "they did."

"How are the roads between here and Mississippi?" inquired Granny.

"They are masterpieces of engineering," said Mrs. Screechfield. "Now we have the big interstate highways. You don't have to go through the towns anymore unless you want to. The roads are built so that you can bypass them."

"I just remembered where I knew that person with

the same last name as yours," said Granny. "His first name was Alto but he went by the name of Running Dog. By any chance is your husband Indian?"

"No," replied Mrs. Screechfield. "He's just pure old American."

"Running Dog wasn't any blanket Indian," said Granny.

"No," agreed Mrs. Screechfield as if she knew all about blanket Indians and people like Alto Running Dog.

"Wasn't any teepee Indian either," said Granny. "He lived in a house and wore clothes just like everybody else. He was smart too. My father taught him telegraphy. Talk about your pure American. One time if it hadn't been for Running Dog the bank in the town where my father and I were living at the time would have had to close its doors, and all the people who had their gold in it would have been wiped out. As it was, Running Dog saved the town."

"How did that happen?" said Mrs. Screechfield.

"Well," said Granny, "this was at the time word of the gold strike at Deadwood Gulch had leaked out and there was a shipment of it coming in on the train that morning. It belonged to the miners and prospectors up in the northern hills and was being transferred to the bank at Horseradish Gulch for deposit."

"That was the name of your town?"

"It's been changed since then. I don't know what it's called now but at that time it was Horseradish Gulch."

"And what hills are you talking about?"

"Why, the Black Hills of South Dakota. Everybody was out there pounding and digging and clawing and scrambling for the gold that had been discovered. Those that didn't have anything to ride on or couldn't walk crawled to get to where they wanted to stake a claim. It was one hullabaloo. Anyway, to get back to my tale, there was a shipment of gold coming in on the train that morning, but about an hour before it was due a gang of jackleg bandits came riding in. I thought one of them might be Kid Kiddoo but couldn't be sure, they came so fast and raised so much dust. Maybe you never heard of Kid Kiddoo."

"No," said Mrs. Screechfield. "I don't believe I have."

"On his horse you couldn't tell whether he was standing up or sitting down unless you were up close to him. He was only about four feet tall. That's why they called him Kid. Well, to continue my story, that morning those rowdies, whoever they were, shot up the town pretty good. One of their bullets came through the window of the railroad station and caught my father in his right shoulder. He went down. I thought he was dead. I dived for cover and so did Running Dog. He was in the station that morning taking some telegraph lessons. I was there just fooling around. My father had wangled permission from the railroad management office for Running Dog to take the training. He was fast on the bug."

"The bug?"

"The bug. The telegraph key. *Da da da, dit dit dit, da da, dit dit.* Probably it was Morse code. I don't know

now what it was, none of it ever made any sense to me. I had no ear for it. The *dits* sounded the same as the *das* to me. Now let's see. Oh, yes. I was at that part where my father had been felled by one of the outlaws' bullets and Running Dog and I had rolled ourselves over to hide under the counter. That's where my father kept his gun. Running Dog rooted around and found it and said to me, 'You take this, and the first one of them outlaws sticks his head in the door you blow it off.' I said, 'If I do that I'll be tried for his murder.' Running Dog said, 'If you don't do it somebody else will be tried for yours.' So I took the gun and raised up just enough to where I could draw a bead on the door. I asked Running Dog what he was going to be doing while I was blowing the outlaw's head off and he said, 'I'm going to be sending a message to the station agent at Onion Crossing. The train will be passing through there in about two minutes and if I can get a message to the agent there in time he can run out and flag it. It don't stop at Onion Crossing unless it's flagged.' Well, that sounded like sense to me, and besides that nobody else was doing anything about Kid Kiddoo and his buddies. The people in the bank across the street had slipped out their back door and were streaking for the hills and everybody else in the town had taken cover. They were hiding."

Mrs. Screechfield had begun to exhibit some confusion. She said, "Hiding where?"

Said Granny, "Under their beds, I guess. If they had one." She lifted the garment in her lap and approvingly inspected its new stitches. Kid Kiddoo and his bandits, Running Dog, the girl crouched behind the counter in the train station, the bank employees streaking for the hills, the train steaming down the tracks heading for Onion Crossing, all faded into dire nowhere. Said Granny, lifting her head to bestow a happy smile on her guest, "So that's the way it was."

There was an interlude of silence and then Mrs. Screechfield made a courteous observation. "That was an interesting story."

"You come back again sometime," said Granny, "and I'll tell you some more." She resumed her knitting. Mrs. Screechfield picked up her purse and went to the back of the house to join Wilma's mother.

Granny said her eyes were tired and that she thought a little doze would do her good. She let her head drop back and almost at once began to snore. Wilma watched her for a minute and then left the house by way of the front door and walked around to the backyard, where her mother and Mrs. Screechfield were hanging the week's wash, expertly pinning the damp clothes to the lines without any wasted motions. They were talking and laughing about their girlhood days in Mississippi, those good, barefoot, sunburnt days that they, incredibly, had shared and enjoyed long years before the coming of Wilma Omalie Lincoln.

Feeling vacant, feeling herself out of tune and out of step with whatever eerie system it was that kept her attached to the rest of the world, Wilma walked over to the end of the clothesline nearest to the house and leaned against its metal post. Interrupting the fun, she directed a loud remark to her mother. "I don't see why you don't let me do the laundry. Granny don't need me to watch her every minute. It'd give me something to do besides clean and water plants and eat and sit." She didn't really want the drudgery of the weekly wash. She only meant to draw her mother's attention away from Mrs. Screechfield to herself. The attractive visitor from Mississippi had gone down to the far end of the line and was straightening a row of bath towels, pulling at their hems until they all hung evenly.

In the act of taking a sheet from the laundry basket at her feet, Wilma's mother straightened. Except for her graying hair, which she refused to color, she looked younger than Mrs. Screechfield. Carrying the wrinkled sheet, she came toward Wilma. "Oh, honey," she said. "It's sweet of you to offer, but now it won't be necessary for either of us to be worried about the laundry or anything else here because guess what? Azella and her husband have agreed to move in with Granny. But wait now, wait. I don't want you to go back inside and show any excitement. Granny doesn't know about this yet. I only told you today because I felt I owed it to you. Can you keep this a secret just till tomorrow?"

"Is that when you're going to let her know?" asked Wilma.

"Tomorrow," said her mother, "we're all going to have a nice dinner together as soon as we get home from church and then your father is going to tell her."

"What if she won't agree to it?" asked Wilma.

"Oh, but she will," stated her mother gaily. "Why shouldn't she? It won't cost her anything and Azella is good company and she's a wonderful housekeeper and cook. And she'll have her car during the days so she can take Granny to the doctor when she needs to go and take her for little rides around town and out into the country."

"She'll like that country part," said Wilma, envisioning her grandmother standing beside a fence on a rural road feeding handfuls of green grass to a friendly white-faced cow. This picture included some faraway black hills, all aglitter with stuff that looked like gold, and a green creek on which floated a canoe. In the craft there sat a girl royally robed and crowned. She held a red, heart-shaped nosegay.

The vision was short-lived and incomplete. Wilma's mind was racing. She was free, beautifully free again, or would be come tomorrow. Except for Claybrook, and she would manage him, she always had. And the freedom, since it was the work of fate and was not anything she had asked for, could be taken without any silly, sloppy feelings. No guilt. The coming of the Screechfields to Timberlake was a miracle and, feeling it her duty to report something great in exchange but unable to think of anything more rousing than Granny's refusal to swallow her medicine earlier that morning, Wilma said, "Granny wouldn't take her pills this morning. She said she did but she was lying. I always count them before and after."

Her mother frowned. "Where is Granny now?"

"Asleep. Maybe I can get her to take them after lunch."

"All you can do is try," said her mother. And said, "Now not a word about this other, you hear?"

"Not one," promised Wilma, and in an ecstasy of thanksgiving turned and planted a kiss on the clothes pole. This display went unnoticed by her mother and Mrs. Screechfield. Her mother said for lunch there was salmon salad in the refrigerator and two sweet potatoes baking in the oven. She and Mrs. Screechfield left without waking Granny. The minute they had gone Granny ceased her snoring and sat up straight and opened her eyes. Wilma told her the potatoes in the oven weren't quite baked through yet, and Granny said, "I don't care. I'm not going anywhere." She snatched up her knitting needles, the ball of yarn, and the garment and with an expression of disdain handed them to Wilma. "Put this stuff in my top dresser drawer and don't let me forget where it is. Next time I need it in a hurry I don't want to have to hunt for it."

Without pausing to examine this order, Wilma went to Granny's bedroom and returned empty-handed. There was nothing now to do except sit and wait. For lunchtime. For the afternoon hours to pass and then the evening and night ones. For tomorrow.

Thinking of tomorrow and the change it was going to bring about in Granny's life and her own, Wilma sat down in the little chair by the telephone table and drew her knees to her chin. She made slits of her eyes and sought a daydream, but her mind produced nothing worthy of development. Mrs. Screechfield's perfume lingered in the room and she seized upon the inspiration furnished by its scent. "Mrs. Screechfield is a nice person, isn't she?"

"She seemed average," said Granny, without lowering her newspaper. "She struck me as the type it wouldn't bother a bit if the person in the next room only dropped one shoe. She'd just turn over and go to sleep. Me, I always have to wait till I hear the other one drop."

"Me too," declared Wilma. This was not true. She had never waited in a room for somebody else in another one to drop a shoe. When she went to bed she didn't wait for anything. The minute her head hit the pillow it was like somebody had clubbed her.

"Of course there's nothing wrong with being average," said Granny. "It's the average ones who have inherited the earth, or they will when the time comes."

"I think Mrs. Screechfield must have gone to college," said Wilma. Her remark was without aim. It was only a scrap of manufactured gossip, a little comradely bridge. She hadn't the remotest idea what a person who had attended college looked or acted like. Both her parents had graduated from high schools and then gone on to schools of business, but there their formal educations had ended.

"If that woman ever went to college she either slept through the part where she was supposed to be studying history or she had other things on her mind," said Granny. "She's no mathematician, that's for sure. Gold was discovered at Deadwood Gulch, South Dakota, in 1875. They managed to keep it quiet for a while, but by spring of 1876 the big rush was on. Had

I been witness to it I'd be over a hundred years old now. Do I look that old to you?"

"You look like you're seventy-nine," said Wilma.

Grinning, Granny folded her newspaper and put it aside and said she thought a little walk around the garden before lunch would take the kinks out of her joints.

Five

Wilma's first impression of Mrs. Screechfield's husband, whose given name was Walter, was not a reassuring one. She had hoped for a positive specimen, one with some soldier qualities, sharp of eye and wit, a person with some confidence about him, somebody who looked like he might have an idea twice in a while and be able to enforce it.

Instead, shortly after twelve o'clock on Sunday afternoon, there emerged from the guest room of the Lincoln home on Otis Street an undersized person with a shy, edgy smile. He had never, Wilma decided, fired any kind of shot in anger, let alone one on a battlefield, and if life had ever violently accosted him he had sidestepped whatever threat had been presented. He blushed easily and his voice was unvigorous. Sizing him up, Wilma determined that he was like the kind who, armed with first one excuse and then another, frequented her father's office hoping one of the big bosses might pop in and slip them a morsel of recognition. She had observed this standardized breed more than once. Wearing faithful and industrious masks, they sat at their desks and performed like machines. Their jobs dominated their lives. A cut above the mill hands, they were the people who dealt with such complex things as payrolls and production costs and shipping schedules, and all faintly and uneasily resembled one another. Mr. Screechfield looked like one of them. Observing his smooth, pink-and-white skin and the fastidious way he moved his hands and feet, as if the very air might contaminate him, Wilma concluded that he was the type who would rather not be reminded where steak and hamburger came from while he was eating and would sooner be throttled till dead than voice disagreement with anybody about anything.

That Mr. Screechfield respected and understood the aged showed in the way he acknowledged his introduction to Granny. When she didn't offer to shake hands with him he produced an indulgent smile and bowed from the waist as a peon would to a visiting feudal lord. "I've heard so much about you, and all of it good too. How *are* you, Mrs. Lincoln?"

"Why," said Granny, "I'm all right. I've been to Sunday school and church so I guess I'm saved for another week."

"Saved for another week," parroted Mr. Screechfield. "Oh, that's rich. I'll have to remember that." The words and his following laugh came from his mouth as if propelled on oiled wheels.

If he's going to live in the same house with Granny he better learn quick to do better than that, thought Wilma. If he don't, she'll gobble him up whole. He'll never know what hit him.

The cool, air-conditioned house was all spruced up for Sunday. In the dining room the cloth-draped table was set with the best silver and china and there was a fancy pot of fern on the sideboard. Wilma's father had excused himself to go to his room to change from his church suit into something more casual. Her mother and Mrs. Screechfield were in the kitchen busying themselves with last-minute preparations.

"Not that I need anybody to tell me right from wrong," said Granny. "I never stole anything. Or tried to take anybody's husband away from them. I only told a few lies, little ones. I never killed anybody or even wanted to. That's my religion and I think it's a pretty good record."

Mr. Screechfield treated these comments as if he might be hearing about some kind of new world citizenship. Widening his eyes and nodding eager agreement, he said, "Yes, yes." He had gone to a chair and was standing behind it. He looked as if it might be his intention to push it across the room to Granny so as to save her some travel, but she ignored him, turned, and made her own selection. To show Mr. Screechfield that her cane was only an ornament she hooked it over her arm and walked without its aid to the settee that had been moved to its summer position before the fireplace. Seating herself between Wilma and Claybrook, she removed her hat and gloves and deposited them on Claybrook's lap. Merely tolerating this liberty, still nursing his grievance against the old one, the child put his hands behind his head, locking them. Granny had forgotten all about the episode concerning the gold coins. Exhibiting a bright spirit of cooperation, ignoring Claybrook's thunderhead expression, she said, "Well, it's family day and isn't it nice? All us happy relatives and friends gathered here together."

Mr. Screechfield sat down, and while he adjusted his necktie, which was fastened to his shirtfront with a gold bar shaped like a paper clip, he said, yes, it was nice, and he and his wife were thankful and honored to be included. And then, with Granny's eyes pinned on him, he plowed on, telling her that he and Mrs. Screechfield had no family other than her parents. He had been orphaned at the age of fourteen when both his own father and mother drowned during a hurricane. A sister had been a victim of this disaster also. A widowed uncle had raised him to the age of eighteen. The uncle, passed on now, had been a fisherman.

"What did he pass on from?" said Granny.

"It started with a blood clot in his leg," said Mr. Screechfield.

"Well," said Granny, "the Grim Reaper is going to get us all sooner or later."

"Who's the Grim Reaper?" asked Claybrook, allowing curiosity to overcome ill humor.

"He's nobody you should be thinking about," said Granny.

Sniffing a possible forbidden mystery, Claybrook said, "But who is he?"

"He's the old fellow who comes after you and carts you away to the boneyard when you decide you've had enough of this glorious life and croak," said Granny.

"Croak?"

"Die. When you die."

"Nobody better not try to put me in any boneyard when I die," threatened Claybrook. Without touching it, he studied the hat on his lap. "I'm going to be buried in a regular cemetery like Grandpa Lincoln and have me one of them stone angels like he's got with my name on it and some flowers."

"My uncle was ninety-four when he died," said Mr. Screechfield. "Azella and I took him to live with us during the last ten years of his life. We made them as peaceful for him as we could."

"Was peace what he wanted?" asked Granny, and she thrust her head forward, glaring at Mr. Screechfield like a mad bull at a gate.

"Of course it was," replied Mr. Screechfield as if he knew beyond any doubt that if the comfort of peace was not furnished the old during their last earthly years they would, in some way, come off second best. His lulling, knowing smile made Wilma think of a boy evangelist who had visited Timberlake one time and preached to a packed tent every night for a week. Her father had only taken her and Claybrook to hear him once, but she still remembered him at odd times.

Whenever she felt guilty or dishonest about things. Like now.

Granny was asking Mr. Screechfield if he and his wife liked the looks of Timberlake, and he said yes, that they were simple people and liked the town's simplicity. Granny asked him if he thought he'd be able to find work, and he said, "Oh, I thought you knew. Yesterday Ted and I went over the job openings at the mill where he works and he found a place for me. I'll be working in one of the offices just down the hall from his."

"And will your wife be working somewhere too?" asked Granny.

"I'm afraid Azella isn't a very modern lady," said Mr. Screechfield, displaying modest contentment and pride. "She's a homebody and we both like it that way."

Reduced to small, manageable pieces, Wilma's feelings of guilt and dishonesty took to the air and flapped off. Appraising the evangelist from Mississippi anew, she saw his hidden energies, his solidness, and the homespun goodness in him and, mentally hugging herself, she thought: It will be all right. He knows about old people and he and his wife will be nice to Granny. They won't rile her the way I do; they won't let anybody hurt her. They are closer to her age than I am so they'll like what she likes. For dinner there was roast chicken and blackberry cobbler, and as soon as she had downed all her stomach would tolerate she asked to be excused. "There's something I have to go see about."

Granny looked up from her plate, which she hadn't even half emptied. "But it's family day. You can't be excused from that any more than I can. We have to stay here till it's over. Then we can go home." Constructing a green-pea necklace around her helping of mashed potatoes, she discovered a bone sparsely covered with meat lying off to one side. "It's the wishbone," she explained to no one, and lifting it with her fingers began cleaning the meat from it with her napkin. To Wilma she said, "This food is delicious. We don't have meals like this at home. You had better load up while you can."

"It won't take me long to do what I want to do," said Wilma, appealing to her father.

"Eat my cobbler," said Granny. "I like blackberries but the seeds always get between my teeth." Like a child just returned from a trip to the dentist, she opened her mouth wide and pointed to its natural contents. "Mine," she said. "All mine. How many people my age do you know can say that?"

Mr. Screechfield said he couldn't think of any. Mrs. Screechfield said her teeth were soft and every time she turned around she was running to the dentist for fillings.

"Good teeth come from good drinking water," said Granny. "When my husband built the house I live in now he had a well dug so we could have pure water. The city water is full of all kinds of slime and trash. One time my neighbor bought some goldfish and put them in a bowl of city water and they died. He bought some more and I told him to use my water whenever he wanted to give them fresh and he does and they're still living. The city water stinks. I read in the paper where it's already been used once. Doesn't that frost you though? Now it's come to pass where people have to drink water somebody else has already used once. Makes me sick to my stomach."

"Mother," said Wilma's father. "We're at table."

Reproved but pleased with her little monkeyshine, Granny said, "Oh, I'm sorry." She didn't look the least bit sorry. She had brought her purse to the table with her, setting it on the floor between her chair and Wilma's, and now leaned and dropped the wishbone into one of its open side pockets. Straightening, her eyes met Wilma's, and she said, "That's for after while. Whichever one of us gets the big end of it when we pull it apart will get their wish." Wilma's mother was pouring coffee for the adults and Claybrook began to tell the Screechfields about his latest craze, a cypress knee doorstop. It wasn't much to look at now. In its present condition it was only an ugly old swamp stump, but he was going to remove its thin skin, sand it down to a smooth finish, and then either shellac or varnish it so it would be something everybody would like to look at or own. No, he didn't know that cypress knees were outgrowths from the roots of bald cypress trees and that the bald cypress was a timber tree. He liked the stump sprouts, though. He liked wood, any kind. He thought when he grew up he might be a carpenter. Could he please leave the table?

"I think Wilma might be excused too," said Wilma's father. Addressing Granny, he said, "Ida and Walter and Azella and I have a little business we want to talk over with you, and the children would only be in the way."

"I don't see how they could be in the way on family day," said Granny. "I thought it was so we could all be together and have a good time. I didn't know it was going to be like this. Everybody running off the minute they finished feeding their faces. The children have all week to do their things. Today I think they should be made to stay here with us. It wouldn't kill them. They might even learn something."

"Mother," said Wilma's father.

"What?"

"The children are excused."

"Then I should like to be also. I want to go home."

"You may go home as soon as we've finished here. Sit up and eat your dinner."

"I've had all I want, thank you."

"You've eaten hardly anything. You want to die of malnutrition?"

"I eat when I'm hungry," said Granny. "I don't eat when I'm not. I can't make my stomach any bigger just because it's family day."

"There are people dying from hunger all over the world right this minute," said Wilma's father. "Don't you know that?"

"Yes," said Granny. "I know it and I'm sorry and I wish there was something I could do about it, but I can't think of anything except pay my taxes on time and keep myself off welfare. Should I go out into the streets and find a beggar and take him home with me?"

"Mother," said Wilma's father in the positive and correcting tone he used on Wilma and Claybrook when they had done some wrong.

"What?"

"Behave. Sit up and eat your dinner."

Granny took up her fork and speared a pea, popping it into her mouth and swallowing it whole. The Screechfields and Wilma's mother were sipping their coffee and trying to pretend that what they were hearing and seeing was only an amusing, healthy-minded little act between son and mother.

Wilma had risen and was standing with one hand on the back of her chair. The authority in her father's face, punishing and relentless, was something she had witnessed only a couple of times before on grave occasions. This was not a grave occasion. It was not anything but Granny behaving like her usual self.

She watched her father add cream to his coffee. He said to her, "I told you you were excused."

"I'm going," said Wilma, but because there was something out of whack here and out of shape and because, for a reason unclear to her, she wanted to learn its identity, she continued to stand where she was, pretending to search first her ear and then the back of her neck for a biting insect.

Into Granny's face there had come a conflict that showed she was struggling for a grip on the treatment being handed her. Proving herself to be still yet a creature of sense and worth and some power and specialness of her own, she again took up her fork and began to apply herself to the food on her plate. There was something almost heroic in her chastised manner. Her smile connected her with nothing in the room. It was faraway.

Forgiving her her naughtiness, Wilma's father watched Granny for a minute and then, relaxing, turned to the Screechfields and began to chat with them about the cost of land in and around Timberlake. "A friend of mine who's in real estate has almost got Ida and me talked into buying a ten-acre piece up on the Crooked River. It's a beautiful hunk and the cost is reasonable, at least it is right now. Probably by the time I retire it'll have doubled in value. What we would like to do, if we buy it, is go up there and start us a little farm."

"The land always calls us back, doesn't it?" murmured Mr. Screechfield.

Wilma's mother said, "Ted doesn't know how much work there is to a farm because he's never lived on one. I have an idea by the time he retires we'll have changed our minds about how we want to live. The children will both be gone by then. More than likely they'll be married and have homes of their own and we'll be grandparents. Can you feature it? Ted as a grandpa and me as a grandma?"

Mrs. Screechfield said she could.

Forgotten by Granny and her parents and their guests, startled because the possibility that she might someday cease to be Wilma O. Lincoln and become Wilma O. somebody else and go to live in a strange house with a man she hadn't even met yet and be a wife and mama had never crossed her mind, Wilma went as far as the door leading to the living room and stood there idly caressing its jamb. She had changed from her Sunday clothes to her sloppy everyday attire and in a minute lowered herself to the floor. What she wanted was escape. What she wanted was to tear out and run to the woods and find her invented friends, but curiosity and something bigger than curiosity held her back and she sat as if chained. She watched the grandmother, who was eating and at the same time studying the face across the table from her, that of Wilma's father. The conversation in the room rose and fell in quiet little waves. The talk had turned to such subjects as crops and soil and weather.

Granny offered not a syllable to any of it. She ate studiously, and all the while she was doing this continued her silent and severe study. At one point Wilma's father became aware of her scrutiny and asked a sharp question. "What is it, Mother? Is something wrong?"

"No," replied Granny in an indolent and puttering tone. "I'm just sitting here remembering some things I had forgotten." Presently and victoriously her plate was clean except for a pile of little ragged bones, and she pushed it away. The contest in her face was finished. She had found the answer, and when there came a lull in the table talk jumped in, leaning forward to place both elbows on the table and to say to her son, "What I was sitting here remembering was you when you were only a little blatherskite."

"I hope," said Wilma's father, in mock horror, "you aren't going to treat us to a blow-by-blow description of that now."

Imitating Ben Frost's foolish laughter, Granny said, "Woop. Woop. Oh, you were the funny one, a real circus. I used to have to run out the back door and lock myself in the woodshed so you wouldn't see me laughing at some of your antics. You hated me when I laughed at you. Remember how when you first started to school what a rumpus it was every morning?"

"Yes," answered Wilma's father. "I think I do, but, Mother, do we have to talk about this now?"

"I used to starch all your pants and shirts so stiff they'd stand up in a corner by themselves and you despised them."

"Well, they irritated my skin and I didn't like the way they smelled."

"And how you hated it because I made you take your lunch in a box."

"I still can't stand box lunches."

"But most of all it was the way you used to eat that caused more trouble between us than anything else. You remember the paddlings you used to get when you'd refuse to eat? It's a wonder to me the neighbors didn't call the police in, the way you used to howl and dance around and scream when I'd try to make you eat. One day I kept you home from school and you sat at the breakfast table till noon, but you have yet to eat that egg and that bacon. When I finally felt sorry for you and let you go you went outside and murdered all my rose bushes."

"I don't remember that," said Wilma's father. Stretching his neck, he had bent forward to engage Granny's eyes with his own. His voice was calm and his face was its natural color, yet, in an instant of shocked recognition, his denial hit Wilma in the deepest region of herself. It was as if someone or something from another dimension had sent her a quick message that supplied the truth, and she experienced a sense of loss and distance, of being pulled and divided. More than all, she knew a feeling of deadly loneliness. Why, she thought, he does so remember that. He remembers every bit of it. The paddlings, the fights when he wouldn't eat, the way she used to laugh at him, the rose bushes, everything. He was only a little boy when it happened. It was a long time ago. So why is he lying about it now?

Nothing in her answered this question, and in a minute, unnoticed by the others, she got to her feet and went to the front door and let herself out. Under the mulberry tree in the side yard Claybrook had set himself up a workshop. He was sanding his cypress knee and wanted to know where she was going.

"Nowhere," she said, "and you can't go with me." She lifted her sandaled feet and lit out for the woods, dark and secret and free. The wild sweet freedom was everywhere and, exulting in it, she tore around searching for her invented friends, calling out to them, calling, "Come out! I'm back! I know you're there! I see you!"

Nothing moved. Except for the swashbuckling bugling of an unseen jay, the forest was still. She elevated herself to a higher military rank and shrieked, "Come out! It's me, your captain! I'm back! I'm by myself! Come out and let's have a game!"

Her cronies of old remained hidden, lost to her, and presently, feeling herself adrift, feeling a deadness of spirit, aware of her unmeaningness to herself and all that had been and now was no more, she gave up the quest.

That evening in the house on Otis Street supper was served and eaten without a fuss. The Screechfields and Granny were gone. "How'd she take it when you told her they were going to live with her?" asked Wilma.

"She surprised us all," answered her father.

"She didn't holler?"

"Not a peep."

"You think they'll get along all right together?"

"Oh, yes."

"Did you remember to tell them about her medicine?"

"Your mother did. Please pass me the butter."

"Sometimes she lies about taking it. They should always count the pills before and after. That's what I did."

"We told them. They know."

"What about my clothes and other stuff over at her house?"

"I went over and brought them home. They're in your room."

"I hope you didn't forget anything."

"I didn't. It's all in there on your bed."

"You want Claybrook and me to go by there to-morrow? To check up on how things are going? It wouldn't take us but a minute. I could think of a good excuse so it wouldn't look funny."

Her father sent her a commanding look. "No. Don't go to Granny's tomorrow. Don't go to Granny's the next day or the next or the next. What she needs now is time to get used to having the Screechfields living with her."

So the load was off and, oh, joy of joys, the summer was still young. All hers, except for Claybrook, to do with as she pleased.

Before she climbed into her bed that night Wilma remembered to kneel beside it and with clasped hands and bowed head thank God for both these blessings. She did this quickly and fervently and didn't think to ask for anything until after her Amen had been said. Usually, save when there was an illness in the family or a crisis of another kind, the favors she entreated of God were of a personal nature, but now, in the dusky darkness, crouched beside her bed, self was forgotten. She took a step toward a new and balancing experience.

First, as a matter of courtesy and also in order to catch the Divine ear again, she repeated her earlier expressions of gratitude, slowly this time and with genuine reverence. And then, in a voice that laid claim to an inner, expanded self, she whispered, "And, oh, dearest God, before I lie me down to sleep, I have to ask Thee to do something special. Please take care of my granny, for she is old and some of her wires are loose now and she knows it and she is afraid."

Six

In his open-air workshop beneath the mulberry tree Claybrook was happy as a pig in a fresh mudhole. This was his time, these were his days. A silent remodeling was taking place in him. Where a little on the dull side before, and lacking in imagination, he was now, all of a sudden, bright and loaded with powers of originality. True to his prediction, his first doorstop was truly a thing of beauty. When finished and set aside on a piece of clean plywood it glowed dark orange. To give it style and a hallmark Claybrook had carved the initial C on its flat underside. Critically he surveyed his finished piece and, finding nothing wrong with it, trotted inside and returned with another knee, this one bigger and knobbier.

Lolling on a blanket that she had spread nearby, Wilma watched her brother. Off and on, for two days and a half now, she had lain there in a strange and brooding half stupor. From early morning till late afternoon the house-pocked street, Otis Street, lay deserted. This was a neighborhood where the staid, older working couples of the town, those without children, were encouraged to live. The Lincolns were the one exception. The houses seldom changed ownership.

On her blanket Wilma longed for something she could not name. She watched Claybrook. His industry was admirable and made no demands on her, yet it irritated her, made her feel herself incomplete. She said, "How many more of those stumps have you got?"

"Lots," said Claybrook, pulling a sheet of fresh sandpaper from a box. "I got a whole closetful."

"Where're you getting them?"

"From Mr. Doland."

"Who's Mr. Doland?"

"You don't know Mr. Doland?"

"Never heard of him."

"He's the one watches the mill at night where Dad works."

"You mean he's the night watchman."

"He goes fishing most every day, him and Mrs. Doland, and they bring back these things."

"How much do you have to pay for them?"

"Nothing."

"You mean they go to all that trouble for you for nothing? I never heard of such a thing."

"They like me," explained Claybrook with unconceited logic. "When Dad has to go to work in his office at night and lets me go with him I always walk around with Mr. Doland. He says I make him think of his little grandboy. He lives in Alaska."

"Mr. Doland's grandboy does?"

"I let Mrs. Doland take my picture once. Her little grandboy never writes her a letter even when she sends him stuff."

"Maybe he's like you. Maybe he doesn't know how to write yet."

"He knows how. He's eight."

It occurred to Wilma that she and her brother differed in more ways than in their looks. People were always giving him things or doing nice things for him. They only saw his pure, sweet side. They didn't know what a pain and a wretch he could be. What a little pinchfist, what a money-grubber. His private coffer, a cigar box sealed with masking tape with a deposit slit cut in its lid, always contained money. He never broke its seal to open it save on birthdays and at Christmas, and then only long enough to withdraw the measliest amounts. His monthly allowance was deposited the instant he received it. He only went to movies when it was a double feature and somebody else paid the admission charge, and he had never known the thrill of sitting on the green bench outside Hilda's Bakery on a nice afternoon downing chocolate eclairs or hot cinnamon rolls.

The sun was past its noon high. Lunch, consisting of leftover wieners and sauerkraut, was thankfully done with and now the long sluggish afternoon stretched ahead. There would be no relief from it unless some could be manufactured. Speculating, Wilma raised herself from her blanket and viewed the finished doorstop. "It's beautiful, Clay. What are you going to do with it?"

"Sell it," said Claybrook.

"Who to?"

"Anybody wants to buy it, I guess. I'm going to sell every one I make except two. One is going to be for Mama and I'm going to give one to Mrs. Doland, but the rest I'm going to sell."

Said Wilma, "You're real smart to think of this way to make money. I would never have thought of it in a million years."

"That's because you're a girl," said Claybrook. His sidelong look absolved her of this sin. "Girls aren't as smart as boys even when they're older."

"I bet," said Wilma, "if you wanted to you could have a real money-maker out of this."

"That's what I'm going to do," said Claybrook, exhibiting a sense of business. He turned the grotesque shape clenched between his knees and began to sand its side with renewed energy.

"If you went about it right," said Wilma.

"I'm going about it right," declared Claybrook.

"A lot of people in business don't make money because all they do is work," said Wilma, picking from some of their father's judgments and quoting from them. "They don't think or figure. All they do is work. It's the brains in a business that make it go."

"The brains," agreed Claybrook.

From her pallet, which afforded a view of the woods adjoining the back land sections of the houses on Otis Street, Wilma could see the old, magnificent trees and the darker-toned understory. Way back in there, when it was spring, the Cherokee roses, white and pinkish, wildly climbed. In winter, when a hard frost came, the forest floor was silvered. Indians in war paint and white men in buckskins had once roamed this untamed and unhindered region. If only the trees could talk, what tales they might tell.

The sky was nearly white, and Wilma thought about Alaska, its icebergs and snowfields. Whales. Blubber. Eskimos. A picture of an Eskimo standing in front of his glistening snow house crawled into her mind. He was fat and his greasy grin exposed teeth shaped like blocks. He was holding one of Claybrook's cypress-knee doorstops. What would an Eskimo want with a cypress-knee doorstop? Nothing. If he got a letter from Florida offering to sell him one he'd probably throw it in the ocean. His wife would think there was something funny going on. Maybe she'd get mad at him and pitch him from his igloo.

But don't white people live in Alaska now along with the Eskimos?

Sure, answered a frosty, far-off voice.

I mean Americans.

That's what I mean, said the voice. Alaska is one of the United States now.

With a governor and everything.

I am the governor, intoned the icicle voice.

Wilma lay on her blanket and pictured him. He

had large lonely eyes and chilly-looking skin. His house wasn't an igloo. It was a regular one and sat on a cake of ice that never melted and where no trees or anything like that ever grew. He was rich but his money had never done him much good.

The governor of Alaska was eating his breakfast and opening his morning mail. He came to an interesting-looking envelope and pounced on the letter it contained. He blew his nose and said to his wife, "There's an outfit down in Florida wanting to sell me a cypress-knee doorstop. Order six."

"What," said the governor's wife, "do we want with six cypress-knee doorstops? We don't ever prop our doors open. If we did the snow would blow in."

"I need something to look at that'll make me feel *warm!*" screamed the governor. He staggered back to his bed and lay there shivering. He couldn't use his electric blanket because a storm had blown down all the electric lines.

"That poor man," said Wilma and sat up. "Oh, that poor, poor man."

Claybrook looked up from his sanding. He turned his head and glanced at the empty street and turned back. "What poor man? I don't see anybody."

"Claybrook," said Wilma, "the trouble with you is you don't think big. You think little."

"I got to get this done," said Claybrook, "so I can start on another one. I haven't got time to think. I don't see why you don't help me."

"Oh, but I am helping you," said Wilma. "I'm thinking about where you can sell your doorstops. I might have just had a big idea. Just for a minute let's play like I'm your business manager and the governor of Alaska wants to buy six of your doorstops."

"He don't know I want to sell him any," reasoned Claybrook.

"Sure he does. You wrote him a letter and when he got it he said to his wife, 'Order me six of these doorstops from Florida. I want something to look at that will make me feel warm.' "

"No," said Claybrook. "I couldn't have done that."

"Why not?"

"Because I don't know how to write letters."

"I do," said Wilma.

So she became Claybrook's partner, the brains in his business. So forty-five minutes later she and he sat on the green bench outside Hilda's Bakery eating chocolate eclairs and hot cinnamon rolls. The bench was shaded by a large lawn umbrella and the wind, coming now from the west, was noticeably cool. "Don't forget," warned Claybrook. "I already paid you once, so tomorrow don't come back and say you want me to again."

The eclair and four of Hilda's hot sweet buns had filled her stomach to satisfaction. She felt good, healthy, strong, capable. She was all those things and their impressions furnished her with pleasure. Yet another sensation, one over body and mind, one that didn't belong, welled, picking and plucking at her insides. She watched Ben Frost come out of the Medical Arts Building, which was across the street. He walked to its corner, turned, and made his slow way to the street and stood there waiting for the traffic light to change.

"There's Ben," observed Claybrook.

"I see him," said Wilma. Curses, she thought. Why did I do it? It'll be like paying for a dead horse. It'll take me a week to write fifty letters.

The traffic light had changed but Ben did not start across the street. Another pedestrian had joined him; they had struck up a conversation and weren't paying any attention to the light.

Hating her gutless conscience, Wilma said, "Claybrook, how many letters did you pay me to write for you?"

"You said if I paid you two dollars you'd write to every governor in the United States," said Claybrook.

"Did I tell you how many governors there are in the United States?"

"You said seven."

Wilma experienced the torment of hope. She relaxed, but the twanging inside her was still only for a second. It ordered her tongue to say, "Listen, Clay, I must have been thinking about the continents when I said that. There are seven continents in the world. In the United States there are fifty states, so that means there are fifty governors."

"Fifty," murmured Claybrook and, like the owner of a store on a rained-out Saturday night who faced his only customer, gazed at her. His eyes began to glow as if someone had just set lighted candles or lanterns behind them. "What if each of them was to write back and order six doorstops from me? How many would that be?"

"I don't know. I can't figure that fast in my head."

"Then go ask Hilda. She'll tell you."

"She wouldn't know either. She's German."

"That don't keep her from knowing how much six times fifty is."

"Listen, Claybrook, I can't write fifty letters for you. When we made our bargain I was only thinking about seven. I made a mistake."

With all the cool sweet optimism of his child being, which more than once had suffered the results of his own errors, Claybrook said, "When anybody makes a mistake he has to pay for it. Everybody knows that."

Obeying the traffic light, the cars in the street had stopped and Ben was coming across. His fellow pedestrian had left him at the curb. Ben shuffled toward the green bench and when he reached it sat down on its far end. He was breathing hard. Grinning, he said, "I been to the doctor. He says I got to slow down, says I should hire me a housekeeper. I told him I didn't know if I could afford one and he asked me what kind of a truck I was going to hire to help me take all my money with me when I go off to my glory. I told him I was going to outlive him. Wouldn't it cork you if I did?"

"It might," said Wilma. She didn't believe for a minute that it was possible for anybody to be corked. Why was it old people always had to use such queer words? Why couldn't they talk in plain old pure English like everybody else? Ben's shirt looked new but it sported several spots and, where the collar of it stood away from his neck, was darker than it should have been. A faint disgust rose in her. She had never been convinced that cleanliness was next to godliness, but never either had she gone to Dr. Bullock smelling unwashed, wearing unwashed clothes.

"So now," said Ben, "I guess I got to scout around and find me somebody to come in and do for me, except where do I look? Who wants to come take care of an old ugly wreck like me?"

"I don't know," confessed Wilma. Ben's broad and foolish smile was a fraud. Hiding behind its lie there was a terrible kind of strained sadness and aloneness. It weighed her down by an embarrassment and a failure that was not hers.

"Ben," said Claybrook, "how much is six times fifty?"

"Three hundred," said Ben, and as if Claybrook had not interrupted continued his conversation with Wilma. "Maybe," he said, "I could get those two been staying with your granny."

"No, you can't do that," said Wilma quickly. "My dad and mother got them to live with her and take care of her. Their name is Screechfield. You can't take them away from Granny. It wouldn't be right."

"That would have been the truth yesterday," said Ben. "Today the tune is different." He leaned to pull up his socks, which had slipped down around his ankles, and said, "You wait here a minute. When I come back I'll tell you all about it." He left the bench and went into Hilda's Bakery. When he came out and sat again on the bench he held a white paper bag. "Parker House rolls," he explained. "Hilda don't make 'em anywhere near as good as your granny used to, but I guess those days are down the drain. Your granny's not herself anymore."

Wilma put the soles of her bare feet together and held them that way. She didn't want to hear from Ben how today's tune at Granny's house was different than yesterday's. She wanted to jump up and run and hide somewhere, yet being driven toward some luring self-knowledge, flirting with it, pitting herself against it, she sat with her face motionless. Claybrook said he needed a drink of water, and she said, "Go ask Hilda for one." She observed that her toenails needed cutting again. They were real and there was Ben, real also. She said to him, "What did you mean, the tune at Granny's today is different than it was yesterday?"

"I mean," answered Ben, enjoying his temporary power, "the Screechies, or whatever their names was, are gone. Pulled out. Left. Quit. I watched the whole shebang through my binoculars. Cut a couple of holes in my hedge as big as dishpans so I could see better. Boy, I mean to tell you it was quite a show. I'd give a cookie to see it again."

"What happened?" asked Wilma. A truck belching noise passed in the street in front of the bench and she had to raise her voice to make herself heard.

"A cookie," chirped Ben. "A dollar. Five dollars."

"What happened, Ben?"

"Those Screechies," said Ben with an odd mixture of sly glee and soured huff. "I was cutting the fool when I said I might try to get them to come in and do for me. I wouldn't have 'em for a gift. Anyway, they're gone."

"Gone where?"

"Back to Mississippi, I guess. Don't quote me on that, though. If you want to know for sure, you better ask your daddy and mama. They're over at your granny's now, or they was when I left my house to come downtown."

"What time was that?"

"Oh, that might have been around eleven or so. I don't keep track of every little minute."

Wilma leaned and grasped Ben's bony wrist with her hand. "But what happened? What happened?"

Ben glanced at her hand. "That's quite a grip you got there. What you figure you'll be when you grow up?"

Wilma dropped Ben's wrist, stood up, and gave a yank to the tail of her shirt. She looked around for Claybrook and remembered that he had gone into Hilda's for a drink of water. She started around the bench but Ben's voice brought her back. "Oh, sit down. Take a load off your feet. Relax. I'm going to tell you what happened. It ain't anything to get so agitated about."

"I've got to get Claybrook and we've got to get on home," said Wilma, but she sat again and listened to Ben's wheezy, drawn-out tale.

"I watched the Screechies moving in," began Ben, "and I felt sorry for them. Felt sorry for Josie too. She and me have been friends a long time. But it wasn't up to me to do any horning in, so I stayed where I was and kept my mouth shut. I said to myself, old Ben did, 'Them two can't do Josie no good, they won't know how.' They didn't either. They didn't let Josie make a move without one of them bird-dogging her. All they wanted her to do was sit and let them wait on her. They wouldn't even let her walk outside to look at her plants by herself without one of them tagging after her, they was so afraid she'd fall down or trip over something. They smiled a lot. Well, now, you know your granny."

"Yes," said Wilma. "I know her. Could you hurry it up a little, Ben?"

"She don't like all that smiling and bowing and scraping and people running after her afraid a little drop of rain might fall on her or she might breathe a couple of germs. That Mrs. Screechie was one of them women can't stand to see a speck of dirt anywhere. She kind of deceived me the way she looked. She didn't look to me like the kind of woman would go after anything the way she did your granny's house. Did you know your granny's kitchen walls was green?"

"I thought they were brown," said Wilma blankly.

"They're green now," said Ben. "Mrs. Screechie washed them. She washed everything in sight and some that wasn't. It was like a tornado had blew in on Josie's house. I finally went over and told her she had better come over to my place and sit till things cooled down, but I couldn't get her to budge. She was nervous as a thief in church and so mad she was ready to chew nails. Last night I guess she had got her fill of it. Anyway, right after supper her and the Screechies was standing in her yard. I was on my porch and I heard Screechie say him and Mrs. Screechie wanted to take your granny for a ride. Josie didn't want to go. She told them to go on by themselves, that she wanted to be by herself for an hour. Mrs. Screechie said no, they couldn't do that, and then Josie went over and turned on the spigot and grabbed up the hose and turned the water on them two full blast. Mrs. Screechie had her hair all fancied up. Part of it blew off when the water hit it."

"It blew off?" said Wilma.

"It went up in the air and flew off like a big yellow bird," said Ben. "I saw where it landed but the Screech-ies didn't. While they were rooting around in the bushes looking for it, Josie went back inside her house and locked all the doors and I guess the windows too, because after the Screechies found the hair and went back up on the porch and tried to get themselves in they couldn't. They came over to my house and bor-rowed some tools, and Screechie had to take Josie's front door off, otherwise I guess they might have had to spend the night in their car or somewhere else. Mr. Screechie got up and went to work this morning, but just before I left home to come downtown here he was back at your granny's. Mrs. Screechie had their stuff all packed and waiting for him out on the sidewalk. They slung it in their car every which way and then got in themselves and took off. Mrs. Screechie was bawling. I hate it when people bawl, don't you?"

"I never pay them any mind," said Wilma, control-ling her anxiety and wrath.

The anxiety dissolved when she and Claybrook walked into Granny's house half an hour later and saw the old one sitting safe and smug in her chair, again dependent on Wilma to furnish her the impossibles, to nourish her with them, to relieve her of at least some of the burden of her existence.

The wrath Wilma could not overcome, for there was the thoughtless and ridiculous loss of her own freedom, her own comforts, the defenses of her own reality.

Seven

And so again in the lives of Wilma O. Lincoln
and the members of her family there was upheaval.
The harried parents said it would not last long. The
mother had remembered a spinster aunt, a lady grown
tired of teaching music and enduring her Missouri win-
ters. This one, a woman in her mid-fifties, was accus-
tomed to dealing with mutinous personalities. Not a
lint chaser, she was competent and her cheer was not
the overdone kind. The idea of a free home in the
Florida sun appealed to her. As soon as she could set
her Missouri affairs in order she would get in her car
and drive down to Timberlake. If she liked what she
saw, she would stay. If she didn't, she wouldn't. Meanwhile, asked the parents, would Wilma mind moving

back to Granny's? Could she manage as she had before?

Wilma minded. Yet when she looked into the two faces before her, and glimpsed there the anguished interiors reflected, she could not say no. To Claybrook the parents offered a choice: Granny's or a day-care center.

Timberlake's newest and youngest merchant, the laureate of swamp stumps, discussed this weighty problem with his business manager a full three minutes before arriving at his shrewd decision. He was a veteran of the day-care center, having spent many hours there during his fourth and fifth years of life while Wilma attended school. Said he, "Granny don't like me."

"Well, she don't me either," said Wilma, "but that's got nothing to do with the price of Popsicles."

"I hate that day-care center."

"When I was little like you, I loved it."

"I'm different from you."

"That's not my fault."

"Whose is it?"

"I don't know."

"All they let you do at that place is eat and sleep and play. They don't like you to work. I like to work. I got my business going now and I want to keep on with it. I'm asking you what you'd do if you was me."

The voice of possibility whispered in Wilma's ear. She thought of the fifty letters to the fifty governors, not a one written yet. She tried to look away from the trust in her brother's face but found that her neck would not turn. In a sad and heavy tone she said, "If it was me in your place I'd choose Granny's. She'll let you have your business at her house. If she hollers at you about it you can move it over and put it in Ben's garage. He likes you. He'll let you."

So the two youngest Lincolns went back to the grandmother's house, under the same arrangement as before. Ben had not lied. Nothing in it or immediately surrounding it had escaped Mrs. Screechfield's vengeful eye. Gone was all its mellowed and eloquent dinge. Every shelf, every drawer, every closet had been rummaged. Beyond the sterilized screens that covered the windows in the room again designated as Wilma's there was the garden, now in perfect order, every vacant can and pot washed and turned upside down, stacked against the side of the pillbox greenhouse, every pathway cleared. Out beside the curb in front of the house, awaiting the garbage man, were boxes and boxes containing decades and decades of relics from a kind of life now done. There were stacks of yellowed newspapers. There was a small bulging trunk with a missing lid, and a round, stained carton abrim with the discards of a human history.

Viewing all this, Granny said, "I couldn't stop her. It was like a stampede was here. Every time I turned my back or dozed off there she was, pawing through all my stuff, throwing it out."

"I bet I could have stopped her," said Wilma. "I wish I could have been here."

"Well," said Granny, "I guess it's time for it to go. It's rubbish, most of it, and doesn't mean anything to anybody but me." From the round carton she lifted a pair of red satin slippers tied together with a length of faded ribbon. They made Wilma think of a wax museum figure she had seen once. She couldn't remember where this had been or who the figure was supposed to have represented; somebody who had lived in France or England or somewhere like that. The slippers were hideous.

"Your grandfather Lincoln gave me these," said Granny, "a long time ago." She opened her hand and let the slippers drop back into the carton. She shrugged but there was an ache in her eyes and, stabbed to indignation and pity, Wilma said, "Listen, you don't have to get rid of this stuff if you don't want to. It's yours. If you want to keep it I'll take it all back inside and put it where it was."

It took her the better part of the morning to accomplish this. Claybrook helped with the newspapers but then announced that he had more important things to do. He asked for and received permission to set up his doorstop business under the trees in Granny's backyard. Ben brought over two doors that had once separated his dining room from his kitchen and then trotted back to his garage for a tarpaulin. When laid side by side the doors became the floor to Claybrook's factory. The tarpaulin would be spread over the whole operation when quitting time came each day or in case of rain.

Just before noon Ben sat beside Wilma on the lowest step to the back porch observing the marvels of Claybrook. "That boy will be a big business tycoon one of these days," he said.

"Sure," agreed Wilma.

Offering his silly grin, Ben leaned toward her. His shirt and trousers looked as if they had never seen an iron. In a confiding tone he said, "I got me a electric organ coming tomorrow. It's my birthday present to myself. Next Saturday I'll be eighty-four. What's your opinion of that?"

With an effort Wilma kept herself from shuddering. She said she hoped she could live to be that old.

"Well," said Ben, "it's not the best and 'tisn't the worst. I'm not on my last pegs yet. I got me a teacher coming too, to show me how to play my organ. What do you think about that?"

Wilma turned a blind look on her companion of the moment. She had been thinking about the Screechfields, wondering what, exactly, it was that they had done to Granny. It wasn't just the scoured house or the renovated garden. It wasn't only the business with the rubbish. It was something else. They had taken something away from the grandmother. Not anything you could put your hand on, not anything you could see. It was something that didn't have a name. Why didn't Ben shut up so she could think? Why did he have to babble so about nothing all the time? How was it that he, so old and sick and useless, could always find something to put between himself and the other— those other ugly facts that reminded him, that must remind him, each time he looked in his mirror of what was on its way?

Ben had forgotten that she had not made any comment concerning the electric organ coming tomorrow. "Yes, sir," he said, "so now I'm all fixed up again for another while. Except I still haven't found anybody to come in and do for me. Say, you wouldn't care to take on that little job, would you? In your spare time?"

"It wouldn't be little," said Wilma.

"I'd pay you union wages," teased Ben.

"And besides," said Wilma, "I don't have much spare time and I hate housework."

"Well," said Ben good-naturedly, "I'll leave my proposition open in case you switch your mind." He said how glad he was that the Screechies were gone and that Wilma and Claybrook were back with Granny, and then took off again on the subject of the electric organ. Anybody with any juice at all left in him could play one because the electricity did most of the work. There was some footplay involved but he could still move his legs, see? The teacher coming the next afternoon to get him started on learning how to play wasn't much on looks but she sure could make that organ shimmy. She could make the drums in it roll and the flutes bawl. The drums made him think of galloping horses and military parades and the flutes made him think of dogs baying. There wasn't any sweeter sound than the baying of dogs on a cool night. The music teacher was going to teach him how to play by numbers. She was going to paste numbers on the keys and then all he'd have to do was find the matching ones in his music book. "Pretty soon," crowed Ben, "you're going to hear some life around here. You're going to hear a big brass band marching around over there in my front room. You like band music?"

"I guess I'd rather hear it than somebody whining about love," said Wilma.

"Roll the drums!" cried Ben. "Unfurl the flag and let the banner fly!"

Wilma had had enough. She excused herself and went back inside the house. It was lunchtime. Claybrook wolfed and guzzled what was set before him without a murmur. "Your stomach is going to think you haven't got any teeth," cautioned Wilma. "It's all right with me if you want to swallow your food whole, but just don't come back in here after a while crying to me with a bellyache."

"You better get started on those letters," said Claybrook, and went back to his factory. The monotonous afternoon began. In her chair by the window the grandmother alternately dozed and wakened. The morning paper, still bound by its rubber band, lay unopened in her lap. During the sleep periods she drew herself back into her chair as if to protect herself from some unseen foe. Her mouth slackened and the color in her face ebbed. She appeared dead, a maddening, unbearable picture. She had not opened her mail, and, except for tea and a slice of bread, had sent her lunch back to the kitchen. Her dress and the apron covering its front looked as if they had been hauled from the dirty clothes hamper. She smelled, actually smelled.

Wilma went to her room and on two sheets of lined paper penciled two letters, one to the governor of Florida at Tallahassee and the other to the governor of Georgia at Atlanta. She had never been good at spelling and her handwriting was the hen-track variety, but she devoted herself to each word selection and in the end was satisfied with the results. She couldn't think where the governor of Alaska or any of the others lived and so went back out into the living room and sat in the chair by the telephone with her knees drawn to her chin. Across the street the trees bowed their heads to the wind; the sky was naked. She observed that even the telephone had been cleaned and drummed her fingers on its stand.

This noise awakened Granny. She opened her eyes and sat up, pushing at her hair and yanking her clothes. She took her glasses from her apron pocket and stuck them on her face. "Why do you have to sit there watching me while I sleep?"

"It's part of my job," said Wilma.

"Are you afraid I might die and you won't be around to see it happen?"

"I'm afraid you might fall out of that chair sometime and break your head or your neck."

"When the angels come after me I'll try to let you know enough ahead of time so you can run to hear me gasp out my last message to my loved ones."

Wilma set her feet on the floor. I've got some rights, she thought. Her being seventy-nine and me twelve don't change that. As if some vocal faucet connected to her brain had been turned on, she said, "Your loved ones aren't going to be your loved ones if you keep on being so nasty and crabby about everything."

The grandmother removed the rubber band from

the newspaper in her lap, unfolded it, and held the sheets up, hiding behind them.

Wilma ran the tip of her tongue around her lips. A queer, cold conflict had begun to work in her. She said, "Wouldn't you like to take a bath before Dad comes to pick up Claybrook?"

"A bath? What for?"

"You look like you need one."

"That's my business."

"Your hair is pretty when it's clean. You want me to wash it for you?"

"No."

"You didn't take your medicine this morning. You want to take it now?"

"I took it."

"You didn't. I counted the pills."

The grandmother rattled her paper.

"Somebody," said Wilma in a voice rigidly contained, "has got to do something about you."

"No," said Granny, "that's where you're wrong. Nobody has got to do anything about me. Nobody is going to do anything about me. Not till they carry me out of here feet first." She began to read aloud from her paper, making further conversation with her impossible.

When her father came for Claybrook at five o'clock Wilma took him into her bedroom on the pretext of showing him a new crack in the ceiling. He said, "I don't see it."

"Because there isn't one," she said. "But I had

to get you away from Granny for a minute. Listen. She won't eat and she won't take her medicine. She won't take a bath or change her clothes. All she does is sleep and look out the window. She won't even go outside to look at her plants."

The father stood with his hands in his pockets, the expression on his face unshaken. "Wilma, I think this problem is getting to be a little too much for you. Is it?"

"No. I didn't say that. I didn't mean that. We get along. There's no trouble. All I meant is, somebody has got to do something about how she does."

"What?" said the father. "What do you think can be done for her that hasn't been done already?"

"She needs something," said Wilma. "But I can't think what it is."

"And you think I can? I can't. I can't turn time back. Nobody can. I can't make her young again. Nobody can. If I could give her some of my own life don't you think I would?"

"Maybe," said Wilma, "Doctor Bullock could think of what it is she needs."

"I have talked with Doctor Bullock," said the father. "I have talked and talked with him. When the Screechfields were here I had him come and check your grandmother over."

"And what'd he say?"

"He said that she was as well as any person her age could be expected to be." Her father was preparing to go. He went back out into the living room and sat talking for a few minutes with Granny while waiting for Claybrook to close his factory for the night.

Her father's settle-down attitude toward the problem of Granny liberated and healed Wilma for two hours. Getting stuck with being old, losing touch with things, forgetting how to live were things everybody had to go through. If they breathed long enough. People can't choose their time to be born. If they could, they would all say, "I choose this time." But it wouldn't make any difference because the years would go by just the same and after a while they'd be seventy-nine anyway. If a hundred million chose the same time, wouldn't that be a mess? Everybody sitting around stinking dirty with nothing to do. Crabby. Hating everything. Nobody young to help them do.

For supper Wilma fried ham and boiled a pot of grits and made biscuits. She set the table in the dining room for two, remembering to provide napkins and tumblers of water. Granny said the biscuits revealed one of Wilma's talents.

Wilma beamed.

"You should write to the army and offer to sell them your recipe," said Granny. "These would make dandy bullets."

All of Wilma's earlier benevolence vanished. I could set the moon on her lap and she'd ask me where the sun was, she thought. "You'd better eat," she said. "You're going to need your strength, I think."

"Oh," said Granny, "it isn't going to take much strength to do what I'm going to do tonight."

"When we finish our supper you're going to get in the tub and I'm going to scrub you and wash your hair," said Wilma.

Behind the lenses of her glasses Granny's eyes began to glint dangerously. "I'm not going to take a bath."

"Oh, yes you are."

"And you're not going to wash my hair."

"Oh, yes I am."

Granny picked one of the biscuits from the plate in front of her and hurled it across the table at Wilma. The tough, dark little weapon caught her on the tip of her nose, causing it to smart, causing tears to come to her eyes. She smiled at the grandmother and with exquisite care said, "You ought to be ashamed of yourself. I'm one of your loved ones."

Granny let a little period of unpleasant silence go by before she said, "You're just like your father."

"I've got his good in me," said Wilma. "What's bad in me I got from you."

Granny lifted her water tumbler, stood, leaned, and pitched its icy contents full into Wilma's face.

Wilma jumped up and ran around the table and grabbed the grandmother. She half dragged and half carried the old one through the house to the bathroom. Granny put up a wild fight. She slapped and pinched and clawed. Inside the bathroom she began to shriek. "Get out of here! Get away from me! You can't do this! I'm your grandmother!"

"You smell," gasped Wilma, "and nobody cares but me. I care. You're going to get in the tub and

I'm going to wash you and shampoo your hair. Get those clothes off."

"The tub's not safe," screamed Granny. "I'll fall!"

"You won't fall," panted Wilma. "I won't let you. Besides, the tub's got safety strips. Get those clothes off and get in and sit down."

"You actually expect me to undress in front of you?"

"Oh, suffering cats, I've seen naked people before."

"Where?"

"Everywhere. Will you stop that screaming? There's nobody to hear you except me. Granny, I'm not trying to kill you. I only want to give you a bath and wash your hair."

Granny stopped screaming. She glanced at the empty tub. "There's no water in it."

"There will be in a minute," said Wilma. Without removing her eyes from Granny she reached for the shampoo hose hanging on the towel rack. Conquered, the old one clenched her teeth and began to undress.

When the night had come Granny and Wilma sat again in the living room. From her chair, which faced the windows, Wilma could see that the stars had come out. She had had her face slapped with a soapy washrag, had been banged on the forehead with the head of the shampoo hose, had had her ears pulled. She felt good. Above the trees in the woods across the street the thin sickle of the moon glowed palest yellow.

Clean and cleanly clothed, subdued, Granny was eating a piece of store-bought bread spread with margarine and apple jelly, washing it down with milk. "This bread is like cotton," she said. "I wonder don't they put yeast in it anymore. I'll bet it came out of a can like everything else. Who are you writing to?"

"The governor of Alaska," answered Wilma.

Granny didn't seem to find this strange or unusual.

"Tomorrow," said Wilma, "when Dad brings Claybrook I'll have to find out from him where to mail this to. How do you spell 'gorgeous'?"

"G-o-r-g-e-o-u-s," replied Granny. And said, "I could make better bread than this when I was fourteen. When I was ten. One time when my father and I were in bad circumstances I did baking for everybody in town. I sold my Parker House rolls for thirty cents a dozen. The society women were glad to pay it too. I had one customer, she was the banker's wife, who bought four dozen from me every Friday. She had at least eight kids and all of them holy terrors except the oldest boy. You would never have known he was a banker's son. He used to chop my stovewood for me and bring my flour from town. Back then you could buy a hundred pounds for very little. Do you know bread making is a lost art?"

"Yes," agreed Wilma. "I guess it is." A little seam in her mind had begun to open and above it an inner eye, not one of her own regular ones, appeared. Twisting and turning, it lowered itself into the expanding slit. When it rose again and reentered her brain it was heavier. It turned its glittering pupil on her and the muscles in her hand, the one holding the pencil, began to twitch. She looked up from her writing and there came then an idea. At first it was only a tight little bud, strangely drifting, but as she continued to gaze at her grandmother, studying, seeing, wondering, discovering, the drifting stopped. The bud slowly opened. She saw.

It was there, her idea, and it was whole, ready to be touched, ready to respond, to be used, to do away with the unused, the unlived.

Eight

Grudgingly, out of necessity, she slept that night. It rained, and in her sleep she heard the water beating against the roof. The thunder boomers came thick and close. Once she woke fully and, with flashlight in hand, went from her bed to tour the house. The doors and the roof were tight. The eaves that overhung the windows did not allow the rain to intrude. In the living room she stood at the windows for a long time looking out at the black, sparkling downpour. Almost, but not quite, it veiled the landscape across the street, moving through the boles of the trees in gusty sheets. The cool and vital smell of it was like a tonic.

She went back to her bed and slept more, and when the dawn came, dry and hot again, she was ready for the day's purpose. Stuffed with its secret, she dressed quickly and padded to the door of Granny's room and looked in.

The grandmother was lying on her back in the center of her bed. She would sleep until Claybrook, clattering and chattering, arrived. The ruffle at the neck of her long-sleeved nightdress, her thin, pointed face, the sleep-kerchief knotted under her chin made Wilma think of the wily wolf in the Little Red Riding Hood fairy tale. She left the house by the back door and went across the yard to look through one of the holes in Ben's hedge. The ex-rancher was on his front lawn broadcasting seed for the hordes of wild and ravenous birds that would presently come to feed. Each time he stooped to scoop a fistful of grain from the pail at his feet he grunted a little, as if this motion caused pain, yet there was a bloom on him. In the rain-freshened grasses the summer insects buzzed and whirred. On the far rim of the world the sky was turning blue.

Wilma stepped through the hedge and walked toward Ben. He said, "Howdy," and reminded her that she was treading on the birds' province. As if he had struck her with his now empty pail she jumped back and he turned and looked at her. "I only said you was walking on my seed. You're up before breakfast, ain't you?"

"I came over to ask you something," said Wilma.

"What you need?" asked Ben. He came toward her swinging his pail. Bent at the shoulders, a little unsteady on his feet, a little silly in his silly rancher's clothes and cowpoke boots, he turned the pail upside down and sat on it. For him the new day was a triumph, a good surprise, simply because he was in it. He had outfoxed another night. His heart was still pumping, he was still breathing. The birds, red-plumed and black-winged, gray, brown, all colors, were coming. He would see them again and here was all this other too, the blueness, the greenness, the climbing sun, life rhythms all.

Seated on his upturned pail, Ben was a spectacle of something Wilma had not witnessed in him before. She could not think of what it might be and, confused, lowered herself to the grass and sat in the attitude of a grasshopper. The promise in Ben's homely, unsentimental face gave her something she wanted.

She said, "Ben, if I could get Granny to bake stuff like she used to, do you think people would buy it?"

Ben gave her his astounded and full attention. "I know I would. When did Josie decide to do this?"

"She doesn't know it yet," insisted Wilma. Beginning to fret, she said, "Listen, it's just an idea I have and I only came over here to ask you what you think."

"What I think," said Ben. "What I think. Excuse me if I take a minute to get my answer together. It's not every day somebody asks me what I think."

"I thought of it," explained Wilma, "because she used to bake for people a long time ago. One woman in the town where she lived used to buy four dozen Parker House rolls from her every Friday."

"She told me," said Ben. "Lordy me, them was the days, to hear her tell it."

"She needs," said Wilma sharply.

"Yes," said Ben, and took a long breath.

"I'm not talking about money."

"Well, I ain't either."

"It's awful. And I can't think of anything else. Nobody wants her to *do* anything."

"You're somebody," said Ben, without looking up. "And she likes you. I'd say she loves you but that might be stretching it a tad."

"I don't care if she loves me or doesn't," said Wilma stiffly.

"Somewhere along the road Josie gave up loving. It happens to people like her and me. We get out of the habit." Ben pushed his hat to the back of his head and watched for the coming of the hungry birds. The promise in his face was gone. He was merely an old, done-for man sitting in his yard. There were no answers in him. Why had she come to him with her question?

Longing to quarrel with Ben and afraid that she would, Wilma started to rise, but Ben, with a quick little hand gesture, stayed her. With a tart expression he said, "Listen here, you come to me with a question and I told you it would take me a minute to get my answer together. I got it now. You want it or don't you?"

"I guess I do," replied Wilma.

"It'd do Josie good to get busy at something," said Ben. "But your idea has more kinks in it than a dragon has teeth. You ever heard of the health department?"

"It's downtown," said Wilma.

"What do you think it's for?"

"They help poor people."

"Is that all you know about it?"

"If you get bit by a dog you're supposed to report it to them."

"They snoop," said Ben. "They got people who don't do nothing but snoop. Hilda's the one could tell you about them. About once a month they give her a fit, she told me."

"What kind?"

"Sis, I don't know what kind. It don't matter what kind. What I'm saying is about once a month they go to her place and inspect it."

"For what?"

"To see if she's keeping it clean. To see if her flour is buggy."

"Hilda has fits? I never knew that. I noticed she talks different than we do but I thought that was only because she's a German."

"Sis," said Ben, "I'm not talking about the real kind of fits. I'm speaking of the kind when you've aggravated. What I'm trying to tell you is things ain't like they used to be when Josie and me was young. In them days life was free. We didn't have laws to cover every breath we drawed. We got them now, though. You take a place like Hilda's. It's against the law for her flour to go buggy and her milk to get sour and her eggs to go bad. One time when she first started up her bakery the health people closed her up for having rope in her kitchen."

"There's no rope in Granny's kitchen," said Wilma. "If there is I'll throw it out."

"In bakery talk," said Ben, "rope is a nasty, slimy thing caused by germs. It gets in milk and flour and bread and can cause people to get sick. Once it gets started it's the very devil to get rid of."

"Granny's kitchen wouldn't get any rope in it," said Wilma. "Screechie washed everything in it, even the walls."

"And there's another thing," said Ben. "If Josie started baking for people and selling what she turned out, I bet it wouldn't be two days before the law would be out here telling her she'd have to have a license. I doubt she could get one without moving into a regular place of business. So, see, there are your kinks, a couple of them anyway. I'm sorry, Sis, but you asked me and old Ben wouldn't story to you. Josie's like a sister to me. I'd do anything in the world for her. Lookit here, maybe between us we could cook up something else, another idea."

"Maybe," said Wilma, holding her smashed dream. She glared about her for something to hate but there was nothing. Ben's regret and honesty were pure. And the birds were coming from the trees, circling, boldly descending. Her idea now was only an opaque disturbance dribbling away to a defeated little string. There was nothing to be done about her grandmother except give her peace and patience. Suffer her tongue lashings, her long periods of remote silence. Peace. Give the old their peace even though the longing to lift them up and give them something else drives you into the ground.

Her idea to outwit, to outdo, would not die. It

only lay still in her mind, waiting to be routed and offered nourishment again. When its opportunity came and sent its thin signal out to her she recognized it instantly and jumped to meet it.

It came at the random of one of Granny's scornful criticisms. During her breakfast time she complained once more about the taste of the store bread. "I wouldn't feed this to a hog if I had one," she said. "Toasting it only makes it worse. It's for the birds."

There. There was the signal. There was the answer.

Wilma piled jam onto her own squares of crisp browned bread and listened to the sounds coming from the backyard. Claybrook was opening his factory. He had learned to whistle. Azella Screechfield had left the stamp of domestic vanity in the clean green and white kitchen, and why shouldn't it be made to work?

Wilma ate her toast and drank her milk and watched the grandmother. "Jaw," she said.

The grandmother set her coffee cup in its saucer. "What did you say?"

"I said jaw. All you do is jaw and whine about bread. It's the best can be bought at the store. If you don't like it, why don't you make your own? You're not doing anything else."

"It doesn't pay to bake just for two," said Granny.

Said Wilma levelly, "It wouldn't have to be just for two. You could make bread and rolls for the whole family, for the whole town if you wanted to. People would buy it. They only go to Hilda's because it's the only bakery in Timberlake. If you want to do it I'll go out and sell it. It'd sell by itself. All I'd have to do is take it to people and collect the money."

Magnetized, Granny said, "I wouldn't want your parents to know I was baking for other people."

And, magnetized, Wilma said, "Well, I wouldn't tell them and neither would Claybrook. We wouldn't tell Claybrook. He's so busy with his own stuff now all the time he wouldn't notice. If you wanted it to be just you and me, it'd be just you and me."

Recklessly and with the raw, hard strength of another, long-ago Lincoln bristling in her head, Wilma began to weave the verbal pattern, the one that would bring Granny out of her half-life and take her for a time at least back to usefulness and purpose and pride of being.

Granny listened.

And so it began, the deceit, the pretense, the designed string of lies piled one on top of another. The magnificent obsession.

Ben aided and abetted. He offered to make an outright and generous donation to the cause, but Wilma, hungering for something beyond experience, beyond her mind-limits, said, "No, Ben. I'll only take from you what I earn."

So each night when Ben trotted off to one of his several beds he left a light or two on in other parts of his house and left a key to his back door in the sack of bird grain on his porch. He drew his window shades and left the money Wilma would earn in a dish on the kitchen drainboard.

And so each night as soon as she was sure Granny

slept soundly Wilma left the old one's house, locking the door behind her, and went across to Ben's. She did not feel safe during the several moments this took. Far off in the depths of the grove across the street owls cried, and there were low moving humps among the trees. In the dewfall and the moonshine the two empty houses down the street were ghostly shapes.

To clean Ben's house was a cruel task. It was clear to Wilma that the ex-rancher had for years only applied a lick-and-a-promise attitude toward the stained and littered rooms. There was rust and mildew. There were roaches, live ones and dead ones. There was downright squalor. The place was more a stable than a home. The only bright spot in it was the clearing in which the new electric organ sat.

In the beginning of this, until some control was gained, Wilma toiled until her body screamed protest. There were some grotesque times, fearful and painful, when she wondered if she might, in some mysterious and emptying manner, have ceased to be Wilma O. Lincoln and become somebody else. Where had her other self gone? By what unknown thing and for what unknown reason had it been devoured?

Now her time for sleeping was never long enough. She began to shed her surplus child-fat and grew to dread the dawn, which always before had been one of her favorite times because she liked its marvelous silence and undemanding vacancy.

Now Granny was always up with the dawn, hopping around in the kitchen, banging the bread pans, organizing, planning. She only used her cane when Wilma's parents came. She was her old self again, bossy, peppery. She was not a really good organizer and had constantly to refer to her endless management lists. "You'll have to run to the store for me as soon as you've had your breakfast."

"I went yesterday," said Wilma. "What are you out of today?"

"I'm low on sugar."

"You ought to plan better," said Wilma, "so I wouldn't have to go every day."

"The walks are good for you," said Granny, flaming. "You're losing that ugly little belly you had when you first came to stay with me."

"I'm tired."

"You wouldn't be if you'd learn to sit and stand straight. That slouch of yours is getting to be a habit. If you're not careful you'll have a dowager's hump by the time you're twenty. Did you tell me Kirby Street had a new family?"

"Yes'm."

"What are they like?"

"Stuck-up."

"What's their name?"

"I didn't ask them."

"You're not much on names, are you?"

"Not much."

"You don't ever think to ask any of our customers their names?"

"They don't ask me mine, so I don't ask them theirs. Mostly it's maids that answer the doors. They don't care about anything. All they know is, I'm the bread girl, and they run off and ask whoever their boss is if she wants any and if she does they come back and tell me and I give them what they want and they pay me and slam the door and I go on to the next house."

"The maids don't ever ask you who's doing the baking at your house?"

"They don't care who does it. They're glad they don't have to do it. They only look at me to see if I'm clean and haven't got some kind of disease. Even if they asked me anything I wouldn't tell them. What we're doing is nobody's business but yours and mine."

"Nobody's," agreed Granny with a kind of noble humor. She said, "I had to tell Ben, but he's on my side. He won't break my confidence. Besides, he's a good customer." She loved the conspiracy and its rewards and had already forgotten that the wit and cunning behind its birth was not hers. She was its brains and its boss.

When one of the parents came for Claybrook every afternoon and smelled the yeasty scents and were offered rolls or a loaf of bread they were pleased. They saw Wilma busy at some little household chore. They saw Claybrook sanding and polishing and quietly exulting in his backyard factory under the trees. He had developed a hunger for mail, which soon would begin to arrive. His fifty letters had all been written and sent on their way. Soon he would be rich.

When the parents came they did not see the stack of baking pans or the tins of flour, sugar, lard, and yeast in the locked cupboard on the back porch. The lard and yeast were always taken from the cupboard the instant they left and stored in the refrigerator.

On Saturdays, when the mother came to do the laundry and bring the week's groceries, and on Sunday, family day, the grandmother sat in her own chair or one of those belonging to the parents. She read the newspaper and drowsed, the Great Pretender.

The afternoon part of each Sabbath was always given to Wilma to do with as she pleased. It pleased her to don her adventure-hat and strap her guns around her waist and go to the woods in back of the house on Otis Street, for it still seemed possible that her friends were there, lost and wandering, waiting for her to call them to assembly, waiting for her to take up her lost command and show them again the ways of the great presiding manitou, that selfless and bodiless spirit of myth and dream.

The natives of this wilderness came from their burrows and perches and watched her pass. They were growing fat and would grow fatter on what she brought to them—the yeast-scented and crusty loaves, the dozens of tasty rolls. They watched her and shrieked and cawed and chattered, and when it was evident that this was one of those days when there would be no human bounty, their talk became irritable. They accused her with it.

"Tomorrow," she promised them, and ran on, circling, jumping through the high, watered grasses, searching, calling. Nothing answered her, and finally she lay on the wild sod and realized that it was over, really over, that other play-life of hers.

The realization purified her. She sat up and looked around and presently with her hands and the butt of one of her six-shooters cleared a space among the pine needles and dug a shallow trench. In this she deposited her hat and both her guns and gunbelt, covering all with first a layer of needles and then one of soil and then another of needles.

This was the place where in spring the ground swelled with the burst of growing things, where in summer, like now, the air was a beautiful blue.

In autumn, in this still place, the vesper sparrow sang in the mornings and, according to his moods, throughout the day, but sang his sweetest, conducted his best services at evenfall.

Nine

The summer was getting along toward its twilight. At night the smell of the coming of seasonal change curled through Timberlake. Its faint and distant voice was still warm and kind, yet gently warned of frost and chill winds, and Granny, tasting it, shivered. "The winter will be here before we know it. Remember last year we had snow flurries?"

Wilma had discovered that the front of her head contained a face and that there were certain things she could do to it to give it a touch of fashion. Lying flat on her stomach in front of Granny's chair, she gazed deep into her little pedestaled magnifying mirror. A present from the grandmother, it was new. The cosmetics on the tray at her elbow had been her own idea. Dime-store though they were, they had cost her almost a month's allowance. She bared her teeth and observed that their frame of artful, glistening red made them look whiter. Her blackened eyebrows and lashes definitely made her look older, sort of like an Egyptian.

Ben was at his organ, his touch-button flutes blowing heralds and his touch-button drums savagely beating. He never thought to close his windows during these evening recitals. He said they helped put him in a better frame of mind so that when he went to bed he dropped off like a shot. He admitted that as a musical artist his talents would probably never earn him an invitation to appear in public concert anywhere.

Said Wilma, "I don't remember we had any snow last winter."

"Well," said Granny, "that doesn't surprise me. Last winter you weren't much of a noticer."

"You want to take a little walk? Let's take a little walk down to the end of the block and back."

"I don't believe that's a good idea," said Granny. "It wouldn't be safe."

"It's not dark yet."

"That's why it wouldn't be safe. Somebody might see you and think you're a movie queen. They might kidnap you and I haven't got the money to ransom you."

"You said I should start paying more attention to my personal appearance."

"You better not let your mama or dad catch you with all that stuff on your face."

"Didn't you say I should start paying more attention to my personal appearance?"

"Yes, but I didn't mean you should get yourself up to look like you were getting ready to ride out to powwow with General Custer."

"Who is he?"

"He was a famous Indian fighter."

"Did you know him?"

"No. He died in 1876, so how could I have known him?"

"I didn't know he died in 1876. I never heard of him before just now. You want to see my new school underwear?"

"I've seen it. Busting a gut, aren't you?"

"Ma'am?"

"You can hardly wait for school to start so you can get away from me. When did your mother say that woman was coming?"

"Aunt Carrie, you mean?"

"She's not my aunt."

"She's mine; she's my great-aunt. She might be here this coming Friday. Did Mama show you her picture?"

"Yes, but I was busy at the time. What does she look like?"

"Nothing extra. I bet she's nice, though. She never got married. One time she was supposed to have married a riverman, but her daddy wouldn't let her."

"Why?"

"He wanted her to stay home and learn how to

be a music teacher. He wouldn't have minded her getting married if it had been to somebody better than a riverman."

"There's nothing wrong with being a riverman."

"His name was Ottie Cluck. He drank."

"Well," said Granny, "with a name like that I guess a little whiskey now and then wouldn't hurt him. Had I been Carrie and wanted to, I'd have married him, daddy or no daddy. She's probably the mousy type, the kind you lead around by the nose."

Wilma was tired of the conversation and tired of the day. More than all, she was tired of the summer. Her sympathies for the plight of the old one were no longer as alive or as intense as they had been. They had weakened and grown stale. Her greed to be a part of something big and important, to create and give to heroic cause, had gone. Her thirst for servitude, which had once been a glorious flame, was now only a struggling flicker. She was bone tired. Ben never picked up a sock, never rinsed a plate. His weekend messes faithfully awaited her Monday night returns.

Her whole summer had been a waste. She was the loser. She had created but Granny had stolen her creation, claiming it to be her own. Wilma was only the attending energy, the one who supported the covering lies, the one who scrubbed the baking pans and washed the kneading board and the big dough bowl and frequently did much of the bread kneading herself while Granny sat and bossed. She was only the leg girl in Granny's high and clever scheme.

Granny was counting her bread money, which she

kept in a homemade money belt. The only times she removed this were when she wanted to tally what its pockets contained, or when she took a bath. At night she slept with it strapped around her waist under her pajamas or nightgown. It hooked in front and was fashioned from stout webbed material. Said she, "I say probably Aunt Carrie is the mousy type, the kind lets you lead them around by the nose."

"I don't know what kind she is," said Wilma. "I guess we'll find out when she gets here."

"She'll not run me and she'll not run my house," said Granny. "If she tries, out she goes just like the others."

"You can't stay here by yourself," said Wilma.

"It would only be for a few hours a day," said Granny. Her fingers rattled the coins in her lap. "I'd be safe. I have a phone and Ben's right next door in case I need him. And you'd come straight home from school every day. Wouldn't you?"

Wilma found that she could not speak. Something in her, a tempest, lifted and began to blow and rock. To the neglect of almost all other thoughts, that of freedom, of deliverance from the responsibility of Granny, had occupied her mind for days. And now there was this.

Granny's question was the kind that did not ask for an answer. For her what was going to happen was already a certainty. Aunt Carrie would come. Aunt Carrie would go. And then the parents, too tired and beaten to argue, would say, "Wilma?"

And she, how would she answer them? Would

she say, "Yes. If there's no other way, I can. I will."

Or would she be able to say, "No. I can't. I won't."

Now in the room's waning light Wilma looked more closely at the painted face in her mirror. Beneath its cheap and clumsy decorations it was not hers. It wore the rigid look of the face of one about to engage in an action not yet conceived. Granny had finished counting her money and the darkness was coming, settling in brown clumps in the street and around the house.

Wilma got up to switch on a lamp and then went to the door. Soon there would be neighborhood leaf fires and the smoke from them would color and odor the dusks, but for now the air was clear and clean. Ben had finished his session at the organ. The oncoming night was silent.

From her position in the doorway Wilma could see the glow from the lights of the town and could identify some of the buildings. There were the hotels and there was the Baptist church with its lighted spire. She could not see the Timberlake Arms, that haven for the aged and the sick, for it was a squat building set in a grove of old trees. At Easter the gates to this place were opened and the old people, some in wheelchairs, were brought out to sit on the wide porches to watch the children of Timberlake scampering around searching for brightly colored eggs. Once Wilma and Claybrook had participated in one of these celebrations. She still could remember the balloons and the music and the way the old people in their porch chairs had clapped their hands and laughed to see a man-sized, upright, pink-and-white rabbit appear and dance across the lawns, whirling and leaping.

The next morning Wilma went over and sat with Ben on his back steps and asked him if he knew anyone living at the Timberlake Arms. Unsurprised and uncurious, Ben said, "I know Flora Young. She don't really need to be there. She's not sick, she's just got nowhere else to go. It's a shame. Her and me used to be friends but the last time I went to visit her she asked me to marry her and when I told her I couldn't take her up on her offer she got downright hostile, so I don't go to see her anymore. Once in a while I send her a box of candy or some flowers." From the tree in Granny's yard under which Claybrook still happily labored, from the woodlands across the street, from everywhere the hungry birds were coming, and Ben said, "Shhhhh. Let's stay quiet now and let them light and eat."

The sun was up and Claybrook was whistling, and Granny, in her kitchen, measured and mixed. Beneath her dress and apron the money belt strapped around her waist was snug. Its slight bulk was comfortable. She was safe, whole again, and as competent as the next one. The money belt proved that. Her twisted wires were mostly all mended. As well as she knew that her name was Josie Lincoln she knew she was never going to lie sick or helpless again, never have another accident. Come the Thanksgiving and then the Christmas holidays she was going to make fruitcakes and vinegar taffy. The social matrons of the town would be tickled silly to pay her price for these goodies.

There were no questions in Granny's mind about

any of these things. The questions were in Wilma's. So that afternoon she went to the Timberlake Arms carrying her excuse—half a dozen Parker House rolls, wrapped in brown paper, for Flora Young. She thought that she would be stopped at the gates and questioned but she was not. In every way the scene this place presented from its outside suggested home. Wilma went across its flower-bordered lawn and mounted its steps and its glass doors, decorated with warning decals, separated and opened.

In the entrance a young woman, dressed in wrinkled white, lounged at her station. She was bored with her stack of official-looking documents. She was bored with the day, with the world. Wilma bored her. Wilma asked if she might be allowed to see Flora Young, and the woman did not waste a word or a smile. Scarcely looking up, she said, "Straight back. Three turns to your left and one to your right. She's got her name on her door."

Flora Young's home was an uncarpeted room that had little to say in favor of the art of living. Overwarm but without warmth, indifferently meager of human want or need or event, its properties were a corner bed, two chairs, a small table, a floor lamp, a mirrored dresser. Its only relief was a landscape painting that drew the eye again and again, creating a hunger to know what lay beyond its pristine depths. There was an adjoining pigeonhole bathroom.

With instincts she had not known she possessed, Wilma saw that Flora Young was the kind of woman who had had things. A home, family, friends, special days, dreams. This showed in the lift of her chin, in her undoubtful manner, in her frail neatness. On the other side of her wall a man was rhythmically screaming, and with a wave of one of her hands she said, "My neighbor."

"What's wrong with him?"

"He doesn't like it here," said Flora Young. Unwrapping Wilma's gift, she said, "It was nice of Ben to send me these, but I wonder why he didn't bring them himself. Did he say?"

"His doctor told him he should slow down," said Wilma.

The screams on the other side of Flora Young's wall were without hope. They did not believe in hope. They believed in nothing.

With iron discipline Wilma forced herself to sit where she was. Flora Young's door was open and she smelled the old, neglected corridor odors. She stared at her hands and tried to think of some pleasantry. "The front of this place is pretty," she said.

"Yes," agreed Flora Young. "They keep it that way. The skunkworks are back here." She bit into one of the rolls. "Did you say Ben bought these from your grandmother?"

"She likes to bake," said Wilma.

The screaming in the next room did not stop, and Wilma's hostess said, "After a while somebody will happen by and notice and then he'll be given something to put him to sleep again." She finished the first roll and started on another. "We had chicken necks and rice for lunch. I couldn't eat. Too greasy. I'm not supposed to eat greasy food. They know it but say they can't do anything about it unless I pay more, and I can't. How old is your grandmother?"

"Seventy-nine," answered Wilma. She was sorry that she had come and wanted to jump up and leave. She sat riveted to her chair while the possible, appalling truth about the Timberlake Arms formed and seeped into her consciousness.

"I'm eighty-one," said Flora Young. "Are you and Ben good friends?"

"I've known him all my life."

"He asked me to marry him," said Flora Young with all the innocence and guile of a child liar who has forgotten the truth. "I was tempted. I'd like to live in a house again, but I have two daughters, and when their daddy died I promised them I'd never re-marry. And a promise is a promise, isn't it?"

"Yes," agreed Wilma, despising the daughters.

"They come to see me as often as they can," said Flora Young. "My oldest is married to an insurance man. Their son is studying to be a lawyer. I guess it's taking every dollar they can lay their hands on to put him through all the schooling he has to have. Personally I don't think he's cut out to be a lawyer. He comes home every holiday. His mother sent him to see me last Christmas Day because she was too busy with her other children to come herself. He sat over there where you're sitting now and didn't say ten words to me the whole time he was here. I had to do all the talking." Flora Young rewrapped the remaining rolls, rose, and went to her dresser and deposited the package there. She smoothed her skirt and said she thought she would just step next door and see if she could help her troubled neighbor. "Come with me," she said.

Wilma stood. The screams coming through the wall were tormented. She felt she could not, could *not*, endure another one. The Screamer was a problem she did not want to see. But there was Flora Young, smiling, extending her hand, gently enlisting.

The Screamer's home was almost a duplicate of Flora Young's. The only difference was that his walls were bare. There was the smell of things long unwashed, there was a level of awareness in its hot, close air that spoke a desperate story.

The Screamer sat at the foot of his rumpled bed clutching a pillow to his chest and rocking back and forth. He was a skeleton, an outrageous picture of what had once been a man. Flora Young went to him and leaned, placing her hands on his shoulders. "Hale. Hale, you must stop this. If you don't you know what will happen."

The Screamer quieted. He opened his arms and his pillow dropped to the floor. He began to cry. "Flora, I want to go home. Just once more I want to go back and see it. I could take the bus. I know the way."

"Hale," said Flora Young, "wait until Sunday. Then your son will be here. He'll take you in his car. If you want me to, I'll go phone him now."

The skeleton lifted a corner of his shirt tail and wiped his eyes. "You can't."

"Of course I can. There are phones in the lobby. It wouldn't be any trouble for me."

"You can't because he's gone."

"Gone where?"

"North."

"Well, he's coming back, isn't he?"

"Not for a week or two. He had some work he had to see about. They said he came early this morning and paid for me again. He was in a hurry and they didn't want him to wake me up."

"A week or two isn't long, Hale."

"It is for me. I could die before he gets back."

"Hale," said Flora Young, "have you eaten today?"

"Garbage," raged the man named Hale. "What they feed us here is garbage, but try and get somebody to believe it. My son doesn't. When I tell him how bad things are here he thinks he's only listening to the rantings of an old man. He doesn't listen. Nobody listens. We pay and the government pays and our families pay but we don't get what we pay for. If our food crawls with bugs we're supposed to eat it anyway, and if we get sick in the middle of the night, well, who cares? We're nobody. They've got their money and we're better off dead." The old man's eyes, dry now, had found Wilma. He said, "Who are you?"

"She's a visitor," explained Flora Young. "She brought me some rolls her grandmother baked. I'll share them with you. Maybe I can get somebody to bring us some tea or milk to go with them, but let's make your bed first and tidy this room."

The midafternoon sun was full and golden at the windows and the old man on the bed sat peering at Wilma as if in her he saw some kind of signaling ray.

His skull's head began to weave as if being moved by some invisible energy and there came his whipped smile and his whipped voice. "They won't let us live. They don't care if we live, that's the long and the short of it."

"Hush," said Flora Young.

The fire in the old man's eyes died. He sat looking at Wilma, aging her. "Get mad," he said. "That's the only answer, that's the only way you can help us. Get mad. You go out and tell them I said that."

"Who?" asked Wilma. "Tell who?"

The skeleton didn't answer. He scooted forward and lifted his pillow from the floor and sat hugging it again.

Ten

That year autumn came to Timberlake as if by appointment with the calendar. One day it was summer, mild and thoughtful. The trees in the woods opposite Granny's house stood quiet and submissive. The earth sighed. The sun rose and set. The creatures in the surrounding midnight forests watched the moon turn harvest color.

And the next day it started, the old stealthy clamor. In the hammocks the pignut hickory put on its yellow crown and there came the surrender of the last flowers. Sounds in the distance were clearer. In full, examining light Granny's lawn appeared spent. Within her house she and Wilma shared a durable truth: They were stuck with each other.

The Missouri aunt had come and gone. For her,

life with Granny had not been possible. She could not, she said, accustom herself to insults. She had, she said, always considered herself more or less shockproof, but the shrieks in the night, the tantrums, the mulish hostility, having raw eggs thrown in her face . . . well, these things were not open to reasoning.

"We're so sorry," said Wilma's parents. "We don't know what to say and we don't know what to do."

The aunt clapped her traveling hat on her head. "Folks," she said, "take some advice from somebody who's been around a little bit longer than you. Do nothing. Your old she-lion knows what she wants and she knows how she wants it. Don't waste any more sympathy on her. She doesn't need it. This child here is the one who needs it."

The child, Wilma, backed off. She didn't want to be kissed by the aunt. She only wanted her to go and she wanted her parents to go. Since she was not going to be liberated, the sooner the quicker. If that made sense.

After the aunt had gone the great miracle of human language and thought laid one of its noblest claims. Only once did Wilma O. Lincoln's heart turn with the hurt of it and then the wonder of it took over and she grew quiet and to her parents presented a stalwart face. She said, "No, I don't mind coming back here to live with Granny. I got to live somewhere, it don't make any difference to me where."

And, scowling, she said, "I don't know why you-all are making such a fuss over this. Sure I'm in school now, but I always come home right afterwards."

And she said, "Well, yes, she might have another

accident, but if she does it'll happen where she wants to be. Why can't she be where she wants to be? Ben's right next door and he'll keep watch. He's already told me he would. And she's got a phone. You could phone her a couple of times a day."

The parents looked at her. They heard the high-pitched chatter and laughter of their younger child. He and Ben were sitting close together on the curbing in front of Ben's house sharing the excitement of a reply to one of the governor-letters. "He wants to buy one and wants me to write and tell him how much it costs!" screamed Claybrook. He wouldn't be calmed. He grabbed the letter from Ben's hand and stood and shook it and shook his legs.

With a hand to his back, Ben rose, and the two went to the doorstop factory in back of Granny's house. To it Claybrook, now in his first educating year, would come every afternoon directly after school. He was making some elaborate plans for expansion. When you're in business for yourself you got to think big.

The parents were not worried about Claybrook. He was solidly linked to them. He was wholly predictable. But Wilma, well, now, Wilma was something else. This new maturity in her shocked them. They weren't sure they liked it. It awakened in them a faint anxiety and a sense of possible loss.

Wilma returned their looks and, because she was prepared for it, it was she who called the deciding tune. And when it was called, the father crossed to her and smoothed her eyebrows with his thumb and the mother turned away, hiding her wet eyes.

The grandmother thought that it was she who had called the tune. To celebrate her victory she baked a cake, and when it had cooled sent Wilma through the hedge to Ben's house bearing a slab of it.

Ben was at his organ, so it was useless to knock. She stood in the doorway to his living room watching him perform and listening to the ruckus. He was never going to change, never going to learn to pick up his own socks or think to take his discarded newspaper to the trash can. Messy old cockroach.

The big brass band, the one in Ben's organ, high-stepped it around the parade grounds once more, the drums rolled, the flag came down, Ben's hands on the organ's keys were quiet, there was a moment of silence, and then he turned himself on his bench and grinned. "How'd you like them pickles, Sis?"

Said Wilma, "I brought you a piece of cake. I put it in your refrigerator."

"Good," said Ben. "I like cake, especially Josie's." He smiled at her happily. "But if you grudge it to me you can take it back."

"I don't grudge it to you," said Wilma.

"Then what's the long face for? What's the matter, Sis?"

Wilma sniffed.

"I been a good boy today," confided Ben in a coaxing tone. "I cleaned the tub when I got through with my bath this morning. The sink, too, so you won't have to do it tonight when you come."

Wilma drew herself up to full, haughty stature. "I don't expect you to do my work for me, Ben. I only said you shouldn't throw wet towels and your dirty clothes on the bathroom floor and then walk on them. It's my job to clean the tub and sink when I come. I don't want you to do it."

"Oh," said Ben, "it wasn't no trouble. In fact I kind of enjoyed it. I went to the hardware store and bought me one of them little short-handled mops. Works like a charm. I don't have to get down on my knees now to clean the tub. And I'll tell you something else I did today to make your job easier. I bought me a dishwasher, one of them portable kind you can wheel around. They're going to deliver it tomorrow and show me how to operate it. Now, how is that for being your good buddy? Old Ben's not the old cockroach you thought he was, eh?"

Dumbfounded, Wilma felt her mouth drop open, and Ben put his hands on his round, loose belly and laughed.

There was laughter, too, in Granny's house that night, the sly, silent kind that enjoins the heart and draws closer the bonds of human unity.

In a relaxed and talkative mood Granny sat flipping the pages of her photograph album, pausing every now and then to give particular attention. "Look. Here's a picture of your great-grandfather Lincoln."

"I can't get up and look now, Granny. I have to study."

"I remember the day it was taken."

"Do you?"

"It was a Fourth of July and everybody who was anybody was in town for the celebration. Back in those days people were patriotic. Off and on during the day they shot off the cannon in front of the courthouse. There were lots of whoopee fights and I guess the marshal had a time of it. He was a good lad, but a little short of temper."

"Whoopee fights are patriotic?"

"It was hotter than seven hundred sins, but that didn't stop the fun boys. Along about noon they got the idea that the cannon didn't belong in the courthouse yard and dragged her out into the middle of Main Street, loaded her up again, and pointed her nose at the barber shop."

"But Quick Draw Lincoln saw what was in their minds and charged down there and stopped them."

"No."

"No? She just stood there with her mouth hanging open?"

"I was in the station at the time."

"Alone."

"Yes."

"Except for the telegraph bug. Which you didn't know how to operate."

"Yes."

"And an important message started coming in on it. . . ."

"No."

"It didn't? What then?"

"The bug was quiet. I heard all the commotion and went outside to see what was going on. I saw the marshal and my father running down the street toward the barber shop. They were good friends. The marshal had his gun out and was firing warning shots into the air. The ball in the cannon wasn't very big, but when it hit the window of the barber shop you would have thought a tornado had struck. The barber was next door having his lunch at the time. He was one of those fussy little men. Couldn't take a joke."

"A lunkhead, huh?"

"Western jokes are different from eastern ones."

"That eases my mind. There for a minute I was worried, thinking there wasn't any difference."

"What I meant to say was the barber hadn't been in the West long enough to understand our ways. He was crazy about hair, though. Anybody's. Before he left on the evening train he cut my father's hair and the marshal's. After that, Horseradish Gulch didn't have a barber for a long time."

Wilma turned a page and so did Granny. On the roof over their heads the wind sang.

The Queen of Hearts and her companion sat talking, talking. What they talked about was not important. The grandmother told another story. In it she figured prominently.

About the Author

With the publication of their first book, ELLEN GRAE, in 1967, Vera and Bill Cleaver created a sensation in the world of children's books. Since then they have broken all the rules, combining daring contemporary themes with the traditional values of humor, imagination, authenticity, and fine writing, and they have received outstanding critical acclaim. "That children's books are richer for the Cleavers there is no doubt," said *The New York Times* on the publication of WHERE THE LILIES BLOOM.

Books by the Cleavers have been nominated four times for the distinguished National Book Award and have been included on such important lists as the American Library Association's "Notable Books," *The New York Times*'s "Outstanding Children's Books," and *School Library Journal*'s "Best Children's Books."

Vera Cleaver was born in South Dakota; Bill Cleaver in Seattle, Washington. Together they have collaborated on 16 books.